HORROR HOTEL

HORROR
HOTEL

**VICTORIA FULTON
& FAITH MCCLAREN**

UNDERLINED

Text copyright © 2022 by Rebekah Faubion and Alexandra Grizinski
Cover art copyright © 2022 by David Seidman

GetUnderlined.com

Educators and librarians, for a variety of teaching tools,
visit us at RHTeachersLibrarians.com

Library of Congress Cataloging-in-Publication Data is available upon request.
ISBN 978-0-593-48348-0 (pbk.) — ISBN 978-0-593-48349-7 (ebook)

The text of this book is set in 12-point Adobe Garamond.
Interior design by Ken Crossland

Printed in the United States of America
10 9 8 7 6 5 4 3 2
First Edition

For Elisa Lam

and for anyone who's ever felt like

just a flicker in the universe

THE LAST POST

An excerpt from Eileen Warren's blog *all those who wander,* two days before her body was found in an elevator shaft at the Hearst Hotel.

Lost in La-La Land
JUNE 16

LA is the craziest, weirdest, saddest place i have ever been.

everywhere i look there are people screaming.

i'm staying at the Hearst Hotel for economic reasons, but the longer i'm here, the more my brain buzzes and i can't think straight.

i swear, this hotel is alive. i keep seeing things out of the corner of my eyes. shadows. faces.

i hear things too. whispers. voices.

the night before last i woke up screaming and scared the shit out of my hostel roommates. i think they asked to switch rooms because now all their stuff is gone, but i hear them giggling in the hallway.

why can't i just be normal.

the Hearst whispers all of its secrets in my ears. it shows me all of its ghosts.

but i'm tired. not scared, not anymore. just numb.

i want friends. a boyfriend. a brain that doesn't see things that aren't there.

i came to LA to find myself, but somehow i'm more lost than ever.

this hotel is hungry. i hope it doesn't swallow me whole.

–E

THE GHOST CODE

Laws of the Ghost Gang, punishable by death (jk). But you will get a stern talking-to by Chase (which is probably worse?).

1. Never go anywhere alone (buddy system!).
2. Majority rules.
3. Phones on airplane mode AT ALL TIMES (hi, Kiki).
4. No provoking or tormenting the spirit world.
5. Never give up personal info while chatting with a ghost.
6. Before leaving a location, thank the spirits and tell them they *cannot* come home with you.
7. If an entity follows you home, let the group know *immediately.*

CHRISSY

" 'Die, you pig-faced bitch!' "

"Damn it, Kiki, we told you to never read the comments." Chase scolds Kiki without looking up from the video he's editing with intense focus.

"Do I have a pig face?" When Kiki looks up from her phone, she's near tears. She's the most sensitive soul on planet Earth. Also, somehow, the most lovable.

Emmaline sucks in a deep breath to suppress an eye roll, her fingers tightening on the EMF detector she's fiddling with. Emma is thick-skinned, with steel guts. She's smart as hell and will go to any school she wants next year. No doubt one of the Ivies.

This ghost detector is an Emma brainchild, just like a lot of our gear. Apparently, this one uses electromagnetic frequencies to spell out words. It mostly works.

"Oh my God, *no*," Emma groans.

"It's probably about me," I say. Kiki's pulsing with energy and I'm already on the verge of a headache. I throw her a reassuring smile and squeeze her hand. It does the trick. Her nerves settle and the throbbing in my head lightens.

Kiki's gained a few pounds recently, and despite the fact that the weight looks good on her, she's letting it get to her. It's not something she says to me; it's something that pops into my head. A thought that doesn't belong to my own brain.

Other people's thoughts often drop into my head like pebbles in a stream. Feelings out of place and unfamiliar, a voice that isn't my own, knowledge I shouldn't have and can't explain.

I run a hand through my hair and realize the reason Kiki's in my head is because I've taken my hat off to scratch my scalp. I throw the wool beanie back on and make a mental note to find a different, not-itchy hat for this weekend. Hats are my mind's protection from unwanted, intrusive thoughts and feelings, from both the living *and* the dead.

Cue that famous line whispered by the little kid in the movie *The Sixth Sense:*

I see dead people.

Wah-wah-waaah.

A blessing and a curse, right? Scares you shitless when you're three years old and you wake up to a shadowy man standing in your bedroom doorway. You're unable to move, too scared to make a sound. After countless nights of terror, you get fed up and tell him to go away. Surprise, surprise, he doesn't budge.

Shortly after he appears, your mom starts taking "special" trips to the hospital with your dad while you play at the neighbors' house. Eventually, she loses all her pretty hair and gets really skinny and sad, with hollows under her eyes. For two years, the shadow man appears in your doorway, faceless and silent. It's not until you're five years old that you finally ask him what he wants. This time he starts to move, to shiver, like you're looking at him through a glass of water. One second, he's in the doorway, the next he's right in front of you. No eyes, no mouth, no nose. A shadow where his head should be. You scream until you black out, and when you wake up in the morning, your mother is dead.

Everyone you try to tell pats you on the back with poor-little-girl-just-lost-her-mommy eyes. "What a horrible dream. That must have really scared you, huh?"

But what they don't know is that now the spirit world has got your number, so your childhood bedroom becomes a rest stop on the road to the great beyond. A holding cell for souls with unfinished business. Or those who die too soon. Sometimes violently.

Unfortunately—spoiler alert—there's no otherworldly psychiatrist to help you cope with all the dead people. You do eventually tell your dad and he shrugs it off as silly kid's stuff. You realize you're all alone with this curse, so you're going to have to figure it out. You try lots of things to get the dead people to go away, to get them out of your head, but nothing works. No, they don't always want your help. Yes, sometimes they *just want to scare you.* The spirit realm is not the rainbows-and-butterflies place most psychic mediums (who are mostly frauds) will tell you it is. It's not black-and-white like that.

So you learn to deal because what other choice do you have?

You start sleeping with a pillow over your head because it drowns out the voices. Never completely, but just enough to let you sleep for a few hours at a time. You realize later that a hat works just as well as a pillow and is portable, so it becomes your number one fashion accessory.

Enter Chase Montgomery. He's cute and a nerd, so when he's assigned to be your partner for a film class project, you secretly jump for joy. Little do you know, your secret talent for communicating with the dead shows up on film. Streaks of light and orbs plague the camera in your presence. Chase not only notices, he also directly inquires as to why that could be. You try to make something up on the fly, but unfortunately for you, Chase and his mom are avid paranormal TV enthusiasts. Chase calls you out as exactly what you are, and it's the first time anyone has ever believed you.

He's also the first person who sees your curse as a blessing. He calls it a "gift." It's refreshing, though you wouldn't necessarily agree. He asks if he can interview you on his budding YouTube channel. The episode gains him one hundred new subscribers almost overnight, so he recruits his genius tech-geek bestie Emma to help him shoot a full episode of what starts out as *Ghost Girl*. You do readings for people and take your audience on what you call "ghost walks" of haunted Vegas locales.

In just a few short months, *Ghost Girl* gains a cute fan base of about ten thousand subscribers. It's impressive, but Chase is always hungry, never satisfied. He recruits Kiki Lawrence to do a reading with you. Kiki is TikTok famous for her feminist rants, dramatic makeup transformations, and viral dances in kaleidoscopic sixties-go-go-dancer-inspired outfits. Not to mention she's got the most beautiful color-changing hair on the planet.

Kiki's terrified yet charming reaction to your talk with her dead grandmother skyrockets the channel to fifty thousand fans. Turns out the people want a cast of characters, and when you're in show business, you learn to give them what they want. Just like that, the Ghost Gang is officially born.

Now you have friends and a purpose.

But what you don't have is anyone who understands. You're alone with the voices inside your head, and not even the scratchiest wool hat can keep them out.

Kiki gasps and it shakes me out of my reverie.

"Come on. Are you looking at comments again?" Chase asks, annoyed.

"No." Kiki tries to hide her phone behind her back as Chase makes a grab for it. He's quicker than she is. As he reads what's on the screen, his jaw tightens.

"What is it?" I ask.

Reluctantly, Chase turns the phone so we can all read the comment.

if i kill u will u stay with me forever?

"Yikes, stalker much?" Emma tugs nervously at the strings of her hoodie.

"It's hauntedbyher666," Chase says, frowning. He looks at me, his eyes worried. I know he thinks it's directed at me.

The problem is this isn't the first time we've heard from hauntedbyher666. The comments started about a year ago. We think it's a guy because, well, statistics point to online trolling being perpetrated mostly by men. His comments are usually about "killing u"—whoever "u" is—but he never goes into specifics. He just drops a murderous load in the comments and takes off. Other fans reply to him in our defense, but he never engages further. It's one and done, and then he disappears, sometimes for months.

We always report him, but somehow he keeps coming back. It's creepy as hell, but it never escalates past the comments, and there's not much the authorities can do about cyberstalkers until they basically come to your house waving a gun around.

"It's just some internet troll," I say, trying to reassure Chase. "Report it to YouTube."

Chase nods solemnly. He clicks the three little dots next to the username and flags the comment for harassment.

I do everything I can to stay out of Chase's head—always. He hates it when I hear his thoughts, but this time his feelings make his internal dialogue too loud to ignore.

Chrissy's in danger.

"I'm not," I say. I clap one hand over my mouth when I realize I've just responded to a private thought.

Chase groans out loud and slams his computer shut. He stands up and shoves his hands in his pockets before stalking to the pool house door.

Kiki and Emma exchange a knowing look from the plush white sofa across the room. Chase's family's pool house is all lush decor meant to impress guests, but we're pretty much the only ones ever in here to use the handmade marble coasters on the three-thousand-dollar Restoration Hardware coffee table. We keep the furry lavender throw pillows and crystal candleholders in pristine condition.

"Where are you going?" I ask him.

"Snack," he says, throwing the door open.

It slams shut behind him.

...

Chase blows off steam for a few minutes and comes back in a much better mood with an armful of snacks from his parents' overstuffed pantry. We gorge ourselves on Cheetos and Doritos and all variations of ee-tos, using paper towels to clean the dust from our fingers so we don't get it on the throw pillows, and wait impatiently for the final cut of our latest episode.

"Genius perfection," Chase finally exclaims, spinning around in his editing chair, eyes a little dilated from staring at the screen. Joy pulses from him like the score of a Disney movie. "Anyone want a final look before I upload?" He's not really asking.

The cursor hovers above the Publish button.

"We know that's rhetorical," Emma says, shooting up from her chair and over to the black bags she's lined up to load all our gear. She sets the EMF reader in its cushioned bag right next to the thermographic camera filter she assembled from materials she found on Amazon.

I watch the little gray bar on Chase's screen slowly edge forward. The video is a teaser for the Halloween special we're shooting this weekend. It's a sizzle reel of the last few months of episodes plus a reading at the Bellagio Ballroom on the Las Vegas Strip.

Most of our episodes are documentary-style, like *Ghost Hunters,* but without the Syfy budget. We're most funded by Chase's real estate mogul father when he decides to take a break from being disgusted by his son's Hollywood dreams. Also, Chase mows lawns on weekends to pay for our travel expenses, and Kiki worked out an influencer deal with an online store called Ghost Tech to get us discounted ghost-hunting gear.

Vegas is full of haunted locales, and we use the Montgomery name to shoot just about wherever we want (since most of the casino owners live in houses developed by Chase's dad).

Our first on-location shoot was at the Sandhill Tunnels, the site of a tragic car crash. We've filmed at the Luxor on the Strip, where too many depressed patrons have leapt to their deaths inside the pyramid. Then there's the Hoover Dam, which has a similar problem, and lest we forget, the corner of Flamingo and Koval, where Tupac was gunned down at a red light. Even in broad daylight, there's something eerie and sad about that intersection.

Chase pops up, stretching long. My eyes fix on the strip of tan skin showing between the hem of his T-shirt and his jeans. He's backlit by the three computer monitors set up on the wall-to-wall desk that he uses to edit in addition to his laptop. I don't realize I'm staring until he walks over to the snack pile and picks up a Kit Kat. He unwraps it, snaps it in two and shoves half into his mouth.

"All right, plan for tomorrow?" he asks, mouth full.

Kiki is already taking off her swimsuit cover-up like business time has ended, but with Chase, that's never the case. Her face twitches with disappointment and my heart clenches—she's right, we rarely *just chill.* Kiki rolls her eyes and flops down on the sofa, crossing her legs. Her newly pink-and-purple-streaked hair sits coiled on top of her head, beautifully contrasting with her dark brown skin.

Chase grabs a Mountain Dew from the mini fridge and hovers behind the sofa, holding the soda in one hand and opening the Waze app on his phone with the other.

"I've packed up most of the gear," Emma says. She yanks off

her glasses and uses the hem of her T-shirt to wipe them clean of any smudges.

"We should head out in the morning," Chase says. Kiki groans loudly. Chase messes with the Plan a Drive settings in the app. "It says the Hearst Hotel is only four hours away as long as we leave by eleven."

We're going to what is quite possibly the most haunted hotel in America in one of the most dangerous neighborhoods in Los Angeles in record-scorching SoCal heat on Halloween weekend, all without parental permission.

"I can't believe you're actually going to go through with this," Emma says, eyes on Chase. Chase is willing to make bold moves for the channel but has never risked the wrath of his parents in such a blatant way.

He shrugs, but he's sweating. "This trip is our ticket to one million subs. The benefits outweigh the risk."

"Taking your mom's Escalade to downtown LA without telling her?" Emma says. "You're a madman."

"We're there and back, just one night." Chase forces a grin. He simmers with nervous energy, ready to explode into a rolling boil any second. "What's the worst that could happen?"

"Why would you say that?" Kiki squeaks, covering her ears.

"We're doomed for sure now!" Emma slaps a hand over her forehead for added drama.

Chase frowns at both of them and crosses his arms over his chest, trying to hide the pit sweat seeping through his white T-shirt. I giggle, fully aware that they are (mostly) teasing him. Chase is serious about being serious, a trait he inherited from his dear old dad, who inherited it from *his* dear old dad— a fact that I know only because I catch occasional glimpses of

Chase's dead grandfather scowling at me from a second-story window.

We all told our parents different stories about where we're going on Saturday. Chase told his parents he's doing an SAT prep all-nighter at our school. Kiki told her mom we're going on a camping trip and Emma told her parents she's going to a robotics conference. As for me, my dad doesn't really notice when I'm not there, so I plan to leave him a stack of microwave meals in the freezer along with a note that I'll be back on Sunday.

Not that my dad would care that much anyway. He's got more of a fall-asleep-in-front-of-the-TV type of parenting style. Also, depression. My grandmother (whom I never met) shows up in my dreams sometimes begging me to get my dad on meds. I always remind her that I'm not a doctor and that he refuses to see one. She's not happy with how my dad is handling things in my mother's absence, but there's not much she can do about it from beyond the grave.

As for my mother, I've never seen her in spirit. Not one time. I tried to summon her myself once with a Ouija board in an attic and ended up with a back full of bloody scratches from malevolent ghosts. (Don't ever, ever touch—don't even look at—a Ouija board.)

Unfortunately, you can't pick and choose the ghosts you summon—they choose you.

"People," I say, drawing their attention to me before everyone's nerves get the best of them. Kiki told us recently to stop saying *guys* since it's not gender inclusive. "It's too late to back out now. The Halloween teaser is up. Our subscribers have been asking for this video for months."

What they've really been asking is for me to use my *gift* to make contact with Eileen Warren.

You see, the Hearst isn't just your average, everyday haunted hotel. It's also the site of one of the most internet-famous mysteries of the last decade.

Nearly ten years ago, after going missing for almost a week, the remains of twenty-five-year-old grad student Eileen Warren were found scattered in an elevator shaft. A month into the investigation, authorities released footage from hours before Eileen's untimely death. Her bizarre and erratic behavior led many Mom's-basement-dwelling internet sleuths to believe her death was not the accident the coroner had ruled it to be.

These Reddit detectives all have their own theories about how and why Eileen Warren ended up in that elevator shaft. But based on her posts and my own experiences with the paranormal, I have a sneaking suspicion that her visions were more psychic than psychotic.

"We're not backing out, we're just wigging out," Emma counters, chewing on her lip. Despite Emma's laissez-faire facade, lip chewing is her number one tell that she's nervous as hell.

"Can I swim now?" Kiki asks, arms folded and lips pouty. Her bikini is tie-dye and matches her hair.

"Go for it," Chase says. "I gotta go inside and finish AP calc."

"You're not done yet? I finished that at lunch." Emma yawns and stretches, rubbernecking Kiki as she leaves to splash into the pool.

"*I finished that at lunch,*" Chase mocks Emma's not-so-humble brag. He chugs the rest of his Dew and then smashes the can in one hand and Kobes it into the trash. "Eleven a.m. tomorrow. *Please* don't be late."

He shouts the last line for Kiki, who is always late to absolutely everything. She flips him off from her rainbow pool float, confirming that she one hundred percent plans to be late.

Chase groans and pauses to flip the light off inside the pool house. He looks back at me. "Coming, C?"

I stare past him at the faceless shadowy figure standing in the doorway. It's been many years, but there's no mistaking it. The deadly omen that haunted my preschool years, that vanished the day my mother died . . . is back.

"Chrissy?" Chase blinks at me with concern in his eyes. I'm frozen in place.

I shut my eyes tight and when I open them again, the shadow man is gone.

"Coming" is all I say.

2

CHASE

5K subscribers.

Started from the bottom, now we're here.

50K subs.

Started from the bottom, now my whole team fuckin' here.

100K, 250K, 500K, now . . . 651K.

I done kept it real from the jump, living at my mama house we'd argue every month . . .

I'm vibing with Drake while I shove socks in my duffel bag. Come on, one million subs!

One million subs mean backers, collabs, funding to travel the world visiting haunted houses, prisons, hospitals, hotels, castles and more. Networking and connections with Hollywood producers, managers, agents, celebrities and studios. Our very own network show! Not to mention the much-coveted Gold Play Button awarded to creators with one million subscribers. It's just a metal plaque with the channel name embossed on it, but I want it.

One million feels like the magical number that will open all the right doors.

We've had a few advertisers reach out to sponsor episodes, but beyond that it's been crickets from Hollywood. Which I guess makes sense because there are over two hundred thousand channels on YouTube with one hundred thousand subscribers. And there are only twenty thousand channels with over a million. We're nobody until we get that *M*.

The second-best part of all this will be sticking it to my dear old dad. He refers to what we do as "that Scooby-Doo gang nonsense" and thinks I'm doing it because I don't have any dude friends. I grew up with two older sisters. Hanging out with girls has always been easier for me. Also, the guys at my school are a waste of space, without an original thought in their vapid minds; they're mostly focused on playing sports and hooking up with girls.

Not that there's anything wrong with that, just not my cup of tea. I mean, the playing sports part. The girls thing would be nice, but I always seem to get friend-zoned immediately. In the girls' defense, I don't really ask them out. I'm too focused on the growth of the channel to care about dating. Plus, most high school hookups seem to happen at parties, and I don't go to those.

I did have a serious crush on Chrissy when we first started *Ghost Girl.* She was so quiet and mysterious with her pale skin and long baby-blond hair and smoky eyes. She even kind of looked like a ghost. When Mr. Sievers paired us up for the TV commercial project, I sweated bullets waiting for her to come over to my house to shoot. Chrissy has no clue how much guys talk about how hot she is when she's out of earshot. (She would probably be a little grossed out if she knew.)

Putting her on camera for the first time, I was shook when I saw the footage. Streaks of light and orbs polluted every shot, every single take. My mom is way into the occult, so I've watched every paranormal TV show that exists and knew exactly what was happening. The first time I asked Chrissy if she could see things other people couldn't, she started to cry. No one had ever believed her before, and here I was, asking flat out. I interviewed her for my channel, and the rest is history, including my secret crush.

I sling the duffel bag over my shoulder and head out to the car. Dad is "out of town on business" and Mom is "having a spa day with the girls." The only good thing about being a living rich-kid cliché is that my parents don't give two shits what I'm doing on a Saturday. Mom won't be thrilled I took her Escalade, but the odds of her even noticing it's gone are close to zero.

I open the garage with an app on my phone (bougie, I know), and Emma and Chrissy are waiting for me in the driveway.

I sigh and pop the trunk of the white Escalade. "Where is Kiki?"

"Where do you think?" Emma has a way of making you feel dumb with just a look and four words. Kiki is late. Kiki is *always* late.

Emma and I packed up all the camera equipment and ghost gear last night, so all that's left is to shove our bags in the back. It's a tight squeeze. I reorganize everything in an attempt to make it all fit. Chrissy hangs back and when I motion for her to give me her bag, she shakes her head.

"I've got it," she says. She insists on doing everything herself.

"Give that to me," I tell her. Chrissy always rides shotgun; it's a standing order since she gets debilitating motion sickness when she's in the back seat. Thank God, since she's the only passenger I can sit next to for four hours. Emma commandeers the music and Kiki is a veritable chatterbox.

I put two cans of nitro cold brew in the cupholders between the front seats just as Emma shuts the door to the back and gives the all-clear shout. We're locked and loaded; now the only thing left to do is get Kiki in the car.

"Does she have an ETA?" I ask Chrissy.

"Three minutes, she swears," she says, putting her phone in her lap to wrap her hair into a messy bun. We decided her aesthetic would be black for the show: black jeans, black T-shirts, chipped black nail polish, heavy black eyeliner.

It works. Our fans love the goth-girl vibe and would freak if they saw all the pink in Chrissy's closet at home. Not that I've seen her closet or anything. Or been invited into her bedroom.

I blare the horn in frustration. We're already almost twenty minutes behind schedule, and three minutes is at least ten minutes in Kiki time.

We pass the time waiting by arguing over whose playlist to link to the Bluetooth. We decide that everyone gets one hour each way, Chrissy first. Chrissy loves EDM. She says it quiets the voices in her head.

"Sweet but Psycho," by Ava Max, blasts from the radio.

Oh, she's sweet but a psycho . . .

"Speak of the devil," Emma mutters when Kiki finally

arrives. She's being affectionate, believe it or not, in her own Emma way.

Kiki emerges like a celebrity from the back of a Honda Accord with an Uber sticker. In her road-trip outfit—hot pink sweat suit with iridescent tiger stripes, bedazzled sunglasses and kaleidoscopic pigtails—she's a rainbow spectacle from her head to her toes. Kiki is our on-camera unicorn and we hope she never changes.

She opens the back door of the Escalade and pokes her head inside.

"I have to pee!" she says, frantic, then drops her giant blue-raspberry slushie in the cupholder and sprints into the house.

"Nuh-uh, she's cut off," Emma says, passing the slushie forward so I can take it. Kiki's bladder is the size of a pebble.

I crank the ignition on the Escalade. God, my mom would skin me alive if she knew where I was actually taking her prized stallion. Fortunately, she's at the spa at the Bellagio all weekend to avoid the trick-or-treaters who come through the Ridges from all over the Las Vegas suburbs. We live in a country club–style neighborhood right outside the city. They turned it into an oasis in the desert that feels like an actual heat-induced mirage from hell.

Kiki loves the pool, though. When she finally gets into the car, she slams the door shut and exclaims, "Yay, road trip!"

I put the car in reverse.

...

We're not an hour out of Vegas when Emma asks me if I booked us a suite, and I realize that I haven't told them the plot twist yet.

"About that," I say. Chrissy shifts in her seat and looks at me.

She promised she wouldn't listen to my private thoughts on purpose, but sometimes I know she gets impressions without meaning to. Like right now. She's giving me a flinty glare. "Please tell me we're not staying in the hostel part of the hotel?"

The Hearst Hotel was built in downtown LA in the late 1920s, the height of boomtown Los Angeles. It used to be a fancy-pants hotel that hosted celebrities and wealthy businessmen. After the Great Depression, the hotel went downhill, becoming the home base for drug dealers, sex workers and the occasional serial killer. Now, to keep the doors open, they offer a variety of rooms, including long-term-tenant ones, more-traditional economy-style-hotel rooms and suites, and last, and maybe least, hostel-like rooms with communal bathrooms.

"Pretend we're backpacking through Europe!" I suggest.

"This is the beginning of a horror movie," Emma groans. In the rearview mirror, I see her drop her face into her hands.

"It's not like we're even gonna sleep! We're there to record paranormal activity. And what better way to experience close encounters of the dead kind than to stay in the room of the ghost girl we want to meet?"

"Wait, hostel? So there will be other people staying in the room with us?" Kiki asks, catching on slowly.

"Yes, other people in a run-down hotel in a seedy part of LA," Emma informs us all helpfully.

"It will be fine," I say.

"This is expensive-ass equipment," Emma argues. "Plus, do you know how many weirdos there are in LA?"

"There are a ton of weirdos in Vegas," I fire back. "We'll

keep everything locked up. We'll stay together. Et cetera, et cetera. It's really just the same as always."

"Whatever," Emma says. She pulls the hood of her sweatshirt over her head and tugs the strings so it tightens around her face, hiding her nerves and her dismay.

"Except we're staying at the most haunted hotel on the West Coast," Kiki chimes in.

I glance at Chrissy. She tugs her black cardigan around her. It's a small move, but I notice it.

The Hearst Hotel is not just old, run-down and teeming with illegal activity, it's also haunted as hell. My mom and I watched an episode of *Ghost Adventures* where one of the hosts was attacked by an unseen force. Maybe it was all Hollywood smoke and mirrors, but he had to go to the hospital because of his injuries, and he quit the show after that.

It makes me nervous to think about Chrissy and how she'll be affected by the infamous Hearst Hotel. As much as I believe filming there will be good for the channel, I don't want her to get hurt.

"One of you is pinky-promising to be my bathroom buddy," Kiki says.

"None of us is going into a communal bathroom alone," Emma says. "But *fine*." I don't have to look to know they made it official with a pinky shake.

Of all of us, Kiki is the most scared of her own shadow. Having one scaredy-cat on the team adds dimension and relatability to the show, and thanks to Kiki's TikTok following, it adds viewership too. She's also charming as hell and can talk anyone into doing just about anything, a superpower that comes in handy constantly. (Even if her chronic lateness is my kryptonite.)

"We have to remember that this isn't any different from any other haunted hotel we've visited before." Time to regroup and refocus. "We're there to tell a story."

"And hopefully not become part of the story," Chrissy says. She turns the music up, signaling she's done talking and needs some peace and quiet in the form of a synth-pop song called "Something to Die For," by the Sounds. We all shut up and bop along to the music.

I wanna hear you say, you give me something to die for . . .

I turn all my attention to the road, trying to ignore the nagging, uneasy feeling in my gut.

Leaving on a jet plane
JUNE 7

i'm leaving on a trip soon. i've never left New York (the state) before, so this will be my biggest adventure so far. I wish i had a boyfriend or a best friend to travel with, but for now i'm flying solo. i'm (mostly) okay with it.

–E

3

KIKI

I don't tell the gang, but I've always wanted to see the Hollywood Sign in person. My mom lived in LA when she got pregnant with me and I secretly feel like there's stardust in my bones. I know other people feel it too. Heads turn when I walk into a room, and it's not just because of the way I look and dress and style my hair.

I've got the "It" factor. I know it sounds insane, and probably conceited, but it's not something I run around telling everyone. It's something I just *know,* and the rest of the world responds to me knowing.

I see the white letters peek from the brown hilltops. I open the window to lean out for a better look.

"They weren't kidding about the heat wave," Emma mutters.

A gust of scorching-hot air blasts in through the window. I can't roll it up fast enough.

We wind into downtown, where glass-and-metal skyscrapers shoot high from streets lined with humans and garbage and humans treated like garbage. I recently saw a TikTok about the homeless crisis in LA, particularly in this one area downtown, just blocks from the hotel we're investigating. They call it Skid Row, and something about that just doesn't sit right with me.

Like the people who live here have been gathered in this place to be forgotten.

It makes my heart ache.

"How's your head?" I lean forward, touching Chrissy's T-shirt sleeve to get her attention. If I'm twisted up with all the feels, I can't imagine what she's going through.

"Don't worry about me," she says. Her lips rise in a tiny smile of reassurance.

"Is that code for, you're *already* sensing stuff?" Chase jumps in. "Emma, camera." Sometimes when Chrissy is hit with a wave of psychic activity, she gets nosebleeds. Our subscribers love it.

"Nah, the lighting from back here is shit," Emma says. But then she sits up and starts rummaging for her EMF reader.

"There's nothing in or around the car," Chrissy says. "Chill." She turns to look at me. "But yeah, it's heavy out there. Like the weight of the sky falling."

"Damn, good line," Chase says. "Remember that for your vlog portion."

We turn onto the street where the Hearst Hotel is. A few blocks over, the tent city begins. There are encampments, communities forged for protection, blocks and blocks of temporary shelters. It's midafternoon, and some of the residents are out on the streets talking. We cross the intersection and they vanish from view.

"There it is," Chase says, his voice tinged with awe. We roll to a stop at a red light.

Chase has been dreaming of visiting the Hearst Hotel since we started the channel junior year. He came to the first-ever meeting of the Ghost Gang with a yellow legal pad of locations, and some short pitches for where we could begin. Vegas alone has tons of haunted spots on and off the Strip. But the Hearst was an obsession—a goal he was determined to reach.

Just like one million subscribers before Christmas.

We all lean forward to get a good view. Chase has his phone docked on the dash. He's recording B-roll, of course.

The Hearst Hotel rises like a beacon. Taller than the buildings surrounding it, with over seven hundred rooms and fourteen floors, it's a show-off of a building even in its super-rundown state.

"I can feel it," Chrissy whispers. She closes her eyes and breathes deep, tuning in to something beyond this world. "It's alive."

Despite Emma's early protest about lighting, she turns her camera on Chrissy. I haven't got a sixth sense, but my skin prickles with goose bumps. I swallow, squeezing the empty water bottle in my hand. The crunch sends a jolt through me.

"Alive?" Chase is breathless.

Chrissy doesn't look away. She doesn't look like she's even breathing.

"It's ready," Chrissy says. "The Hearst is ready to meet us."

"Jesus Christ." Emma's voice shakes.

The light turns green, but Chase doesn't accelerate. He's staring, transfixed, at Chrissy's profile. Until car horns blare behind us, and we lurch forward, a little slower than before.

...

EMMALINE

I gotta admit, that show of Chrissy's freaked me the hell out. And I do not freak out.

As a rule, I approach hauntings with a hefty dose of skepticism.

Science first, feelings never, if I had my way. It's not that I don't buy the I-see-dead-people thing. Albert Einstein, Thomas Edison, Alan Turing—some of the greatest thinkers of all time believed in the supernatural, in worlds beyond, in ESP. And even if you can't prove its existence, you also can't disprove it. Thereby, we must stay open to all possibilities. It's what good scientists do.

Agnosticism is the soul of science.

It's just that the theatrics of psychic phenomena always feel a little sketch to me. I like data. Proof in a form that isn't tainted by the human factor. No matter how real the power is, the data never lies.

Still. This place gives me a stomachache and we're only standing outside.

"It's pretty," Kiki says.

I snort. "It's a dump."

"Don't say that," Kiki says. "What if it's listening?" She is not making a joke, either. Kiki not only one hundred percent believes in every single mystical force of the universe, but she also feels every single feeling with acute authenticity. And she is scared shitless. I can read it on her face, no sixth sense required.

"Grab that bag, will you?" I ask her, brushing past her fear.

Chase runs up, out of breath. "All right, car is parked." His eyes travel over to Chrissy.

She hasn't moved since we got out of the Escalade. Not even when I asked her to grab her stuff from the curb so we could at least get inside the hotel and off this godforsaken street that smells strongly of pee.

Chase motions for me to hand him his Canon Rebel. I clench my jaw and shake my head once. *No. Not out here.* He settles for the camera on his phone instead.

"Chrissy, tell us what you're seeing," he says. His voice is steady, soothing in a way that I know he's practiced for moments just like this. Thing is, I don't think he totally has to practice being extra sensitive to Chrissy.

"It's shimmering," she says, her voice low. "Like the hotel itself isn't all here all at once, all at the same time."

Chase slides his phone up to film the length of the Hearst Hotel's lean body. It won't show us what Chrissy sees. Nothing can, not even my thermal filter. This is the kind of picture she has to paint for our viewers, and despite the lack of proof, they devour it like cake for breakfast.

"This isn't just any haunted hotel," she says. "This place is . . . different." She glances at the camera and then looks at Chase, who is still busy capturing footage of the hotel. "It's not going to let us go without a show."

Chase fist-pumps without looking away from his phone, so he doesn't see that Chrissy is frowning when she says it.

Chrissy walks toward the doors, her black combat boots crunching gravel on the cement. It's like she's in a trance, being pulled inside by an invisible string. Chase ends the video he's recording and lowers his phone, staring after her. Concern finally catches up with him, and his brows scrunch together. Kiki rushes up to take Chrissy by the hand.

"You wanted a million subs," I say, passing Chase. "Buckle up, buttercup."

I push through the revolving doors, leaving Chase outside to grab his and Chrissy's duffel bags.

The lobby is ornate, if a little shabby after years of wear and tear and no updates or renovations. By the entrance, there's a giant clock with an elaborate gold metal sunburst around its face. The clock reads 4:16 and ticks loudly. The floors are marble with no obvious signs of erosion, despite years of foot traffic. Even though it's clean enough and objectively beautiful with its art deco design, the hotel feels unloved. It's more than just old and outdated—beneath all this marble, wrought iron and stained glass, its soul is rotting.

To the left is a stairwell that leads down to another level of the lobby. Straight ahead is the front desk, backed by a set of green-and-gold shelves, the kind you'd expect in a hotel built in the '20s. Chase walks past me, lugging bags.

He drops them at Chrissy's and Kiki's feet. Kiki has her phone up and is filming something on the Ghost Gang Tik-Tok, which she has single-handedly built up to almost one hundred thousand followers. She's driving traffic to our YouTube channel, too, even if right now a lot of them just watch for her pretty, not-at-all-piggish face.

I sit beside Chrissy on the couch. Dust puffs out around us.

"It definitely *looks* haunted," I say, nudging Chrissy with my elbow a few times.

Chrissy has a finger pressed between her eyes, but she exhales a laugh.

Chase approaches the front desk, a smile painted on his face. Kiki gets a whiff of him trying to interact with a person and follows.

"Are you going to be okay?" I ask Chrissy. Her face is green. "You look nauseated."

"Yeah, yeah," she says, sucking air in through her nose. "I'm good. Maybe I'm just hungry."

"Oh, is it hunger that's making you all pale and sweaty," I ask, "and not the trapped souls of the lost and the damned?"

She points, asking for a water bottle from the bag of snacks that Kiki packed. I hand it over, along with a bag of Cheez-Its.

Chrissy takes a massive swig of water and starts to wrestle the bag of crackers open but stops. Her eyes go wide, and she cranes her neck to look at the front desk, where Chase is checking us into the hotel.

"What is it?" I ask her. "What do you see now?" She zones out for a solid minute before coming back to earth.

She shakes her head and pops open the bag, then shoves a square into her mouth.

"The dead aren't the only problem around here."

...

CHASE

Steve. His name is Steve, and his shiny bald spot reflects the light, blinding me in the left eye. His beady-eyed gaze shifts from me to Kiki, then to Chrissy and Emma on the couch, and every single time his watery gray eyes narrow a millimeter more.

"We're gonna pay in cash," I say. Dad regularly checks my bank account, so this whole trip has to be funded with the cash from a collab that Kiki got for us with *Ghastly Gore* movie makeup. (Kiki is the queen of securing lucrative deals with brands. She doesn't think of herself as our manager, but I wouldn't be opposed to her having the title if she wanted it.)

"You kids are all eighteen?" Steve asks. His eyes slide over me. I feel slimed.

"This is my birthday weekend," Kiki says. It's not. He turns his sallow glare on her.

He can't ask for IDs since we're paying in cash and I provided one already. I'm paying; I'm the one listed on the registration; I'm eighteen. Which is basically useless in a home like mine, where I still get treated like the baby.

A blond woman approaches. *Linda.* The name tag on her collar is crooked and she's got heavy bags under her bulging eyes. Her hair is a nest not even rats would want to call home.

Her smile is crooked, yellowish and amoral.

"Give them the keys, dear," she says, rubbing Steve's back to calm him down. She takes the wad of cash from my hands, straightening the bills as she counts them.

Dear? My eyes dart down to their fingers. No rings, so not married. Plus, she's at least twenty years his senior. I quickglance at their faces. Same pallid complexion, hooked noses, tiny discolored teeth that show when they impersonate smiling. The family resemblance is clear.

I get strong Hitchcock vibes, Norma and Norman Bates from *Psycho,* and my brain shows me Linda in a rocking chair, her flesh melting off her bones.

Ugh.

Steve swallows and turns to face me, disgust twisting his features.

"Prepare for rolling blackouts all night," he says. "Heat, traffic, Halloween—you get it." He flicks his eyes from me to Kiki again. She flashes a disarming smile. His lips curl involuntarily, showing more gum than teeth.

He quickly alters his expression and writes down our room number on the key sleeve. "Room 421." He sets the pen down and waves the paper sleeve at us, reveling in his *gotcha* moment. "You're here because of Eileen Warren."

Linda looks up.

"Actually, we're going to a concert at the Hollywood Bowl," I say, evading the question with well-rehearsed mastery. Thank you, Eventbrite. "Classic horror movie soundtracks played by an orchestra. Ever been?" I show them my teeth with a smile.

"*Jaws* is my favorite," Kiki says. "Da-dum. Da-dum—" She giggles.

"Great." Linda's voice is joyless. "There's a bus that goes to the Hollywood Bowl, stops right outside. Have fun."

Linda wrestles the sleeve away from Steve and drops four keys into the flimsy parchment envelope before handing it over to me. "Fifty bucks per key if you lose 'em," she says, delighted at the possibility of squeezing more money out of us.

I feel Steve's narrowed, livid gaze on us as we walk away. A chill runs down my spine. What the hell is that guy's problem?

Chrissy's eyes meet mine as we descend the steps with our

gear and bags and then cross the lower level of the lobby toward the bank of elevators. She's moving slow. Extra slow. Painfully slow.

"Do you need me to take your bag?" I ask. She shakes her head.

"I'm fine," she says, powering along with her heavy duffel and what I can only assume is a massive psychic headache. She gets them sometimes when we go to places with a lot of history. Violent history especially. They're called "psychic attacks"— I've Googled them. I bring Motrin with me everywhere we go, and Kiki always has the herbal and homeopathic tinctures on lock.

Chrissy winces and tries to keep up with me. "We need to watch out for those two. Something is not right about them."

She nods her head in the direction of the front desk. Linda has disappeared into the back. Steve is watching, his greasy hair framing his belligerent gaze.

"Yeah, no kidding," I say, shrugging.

"No, I mean it, Chase," Chrissy says, wrapping her free hand around my wrist to emphasize her point. "Their auras are black."

The heat from Chrissy's touch travels all the way up my arm and into my face, and I pull away so she can't see my red ears. Blood on Steve's and Linda's hands is creepy, but not nearly as creepy as what I just imagined me and Chrissy doing.

"Okay, okay" is all I say, trying to shake the image out of my head. "We'll be careful, I promise."

She watches me, confused, so I try to clear my head of anything incriminating. My brain decides to show me Norma Bates's rotting corpse again, and that does the trick.

When we get to the elevator, we gather in front of it and stare like it's a cursed object.

"You do it, Chase," Emma says. I press the little metal button and it lights up. We listen as the elevator slowly glides down.

In a hotel like the Hearst, the elevator would be a horror story all on its own, but the fact that Eileen Warren was found dead in this very elevator shaft makes it eerie to even look at, let alone get inside.

The *ding* is full-bodied, and the gilded doors open wide.

...

CHRISSY

Everywhere I look, it's a nightmare.

Shadows move in the periphery of my vision. The patterns in the art deco wallpaper shift and distort into figures and faces. I see dead bodies by the dozens carried out on stretchers and covered in white sheets. One hundred years of history pulse inside my head as if everything is happening right now and all at once.

It's almost as if the hotel is a sentient being—alive and tormenting me.

Blood drips down the elevator doors and pools over the tile floor of the lobby. The doors open, and it's raining blood, staining the carpet and mirrored walls inside the elevator car.

I don't want to. I don't want to go in.

Chase, Kiki and Emma step inside the elevator. Drops of dark red blood soak their hair, their skin, their clothes. They

36

turn to face me, covered in brain matter that catches in their hair and clothes.

It's not there, it's not really there.

I'm the only one who sees the blood. I know that, but it doesn't make it less real. The hotel and spirits that reside within it are issuing a warning. It's one part *stay away* and two parts *come and play.*

The hotel is aware of my presence and more than anything it wants to tell me its story. It knows there's something different about me. Something it can use to entertain itself. Someone to show off to.

"Chrissy?" Chase looks concerned. Emma holds down the Door Open button, waiting for me to join them. They are no longer bathed in blood, but the eerie feeling remains.

I take a deep breath and step inside. Emma presses the button for the fourth floor.

It's ice cold in the elevator. I pull my sweater in around me. *Do they feel it?*

Chase has already started filming. I blink, trying to clear my vision, but the pounding in my head crashes through me. Shards of glass poke behind my eyes; cold steel tightens down my spine.

The air is heavy, laden with the metallic scent of rust and rotten eggs.

It's the smell of blood. The sulfurous stench of something rotting.

I taste it on my tongue. Iron and water mixed with death.

"What is it?" Kiki's voice is the beaming light from a house set up on the shore. I'm a ship coming in from a storm.

"Someone is in here," I say, shivering.

"I have a list of ghosts that are known to interact in this elevator," Emma says. I hear the rustle of her clothing as she pulls her phone out.

I close my eyes, trying to fight the wave of nausea crescendoing through my guts.

"It's legit cold in here," Kiki again. "Is this Eileen?"

"Is it Eileen?" Chase says. He edges nearer to me. I feel the heat of his body, smell his deodorant, all earthy pungent spice. It grounds me, nudging me out of this waking nightmare.

"Is there anything you can tell us?" Chase asks me.

The elevator dings and lurches to a stop. The doors slide open.

I stumble out and vomit all over the carpet.

MARCH 18

I see dead people. I'M THAT BITCH!

    –E

4

CHRISSY

"Oh my God." I hear Kiki's voice behind me. My head pounds, my brain is mush. All I can think about is that it's going to happen again.

I step over my puke and drop my duffel bag. I look down the hall in both directions. At the far end is the bathroom.

The hallway yawns. Expands. Like lungs inhaling, exhaling.

My feet are concrete blocks, but I manage to run.

"I'm coming!" Emma yells, and I hear her footsteps behind me. They sound further away than they should.

Other footsteps. *Chase.* "You're not filming this." Emma almost growls out the words. A panther friend, not to be trifled with.

"I'll stand outside the stall," he offers.

"No chance in *hell.*" Emma is firm.

I twist the metal handle on the bathroom door and launch myself inside.

It's like a locker room. Dingy gray tiles with moldy grout.

On one side, a row of showers; on the other, a row of toilet stalls. In the center, a bank of sinks.

I practically swan dive into the cleanest-looking stall. My knees hit the cool gritty tile, which cuts into my skin through the rips in my jeans. My fingers spread across the white ceramic toilet bowl. I feel Emma's presence behind me. Her fingers twist in my hair to hold it back.

I puke up water and what's left of the In-N-Out burger I had on the road.

"In and right back out," Emma says, trying not to gag at the smell of regurgitated fast food. The thought of lunch makes me heave and cough again, but nothing else comes out.

I close my eyes, focus on my breathing and lean away from the toilet. I pull the lever, flushing the contents of my stomach. I open my eyes and try to focus on the line where the ugly gray tile turns to boring beige wall.

Out of the corner of my eye, I see movement under the stall next to mine.

My stomach drops. There was no one in this bathroom when we came in.

I hear a moan.

"I'll get paper towels," Emma says. She doesn't seem to hear anything, which can only mean one thing.

I swallow the raw lump in my throat and dip my head down slowly, until I can see under the dividing parition. A pair of bare feet come into view. They are purple and blue and shuffling back and forth nervously. A shaky hand holds a dirty needle and I can only guess what comes next. I squeeze my eyes shut.

"Emma . . . ," I say, suddenly wanting to get the hell out of this bathroom, but with no strength to lift myself off the floor.

The occupant slams into the wall between us and slumps to the ground, convulsing. When I open my eyes, her stringy long brown hair is fanned out around her and into my stall. After a few seconds of violent shaking and contorting, her body goes completely still. I breathe a sigh of relief.

Sometimes they like to show me how they died. I don't know why, maybe it makes them feel less alone, less isolated. Maybe they just want someone to know, to witness it, so it gives their short life meaning. Usually they show me and then vanish. Sometimes they don't know I'm there, or even seem to realize they are. It's like they're caught in this endless loop of their last living moments, and I'm just an audience to the horror. One they can't see or maybe don't want to acknowledge.

I wait, but she doesn't disappear. She lies there, bruised, mangled from misuse and lifeless. I start to fear she's not a ghost after all, so I do something I never do. I reach out to touch her. To make sure she's an apparition and not a real person in need of help.

A bony white hand snatches my wrist like a spider capturing prey.

I clamp my mouth shut to suppress the scream rising in my chest.

Her invisible grip is somehow so tight it hurts. She pulls me toward her. I try to pull away, tears streaming down my face, but her dirt-caked nails dig into my skin.

Her eyes are cloudy with decay. Her dry, cracked lips whisper words I can't hear and don't understand. I close my eyes, and suddenly the whisper is right next to my ear.

You'll die too.

"Here you go." Emma's voice startles me. My eyes fly open

and she is reaching down with paper towels in front of my face. I push myself up from the ground.

"Are you okay?" She cocks her head.

"This isn't going to work," I say. "Something bad is going to happen." I'm shaking my head, driving headlong into a full-blown panic attack.

Emma takes in a deep breath and sets the paper towels down. My friends always ask me if I'm okay, and usually I am. This time, though, is different.

"I want to try something," Emma says. She reaches up, pulls off her dark green beanie and places it on top of the black hat I'm wearing. Immediately, all the noise that doesn't belong to me is muffled. It's replaced by the stern, clear focused feeling I've come to associate with one of my best friends.

"Better?" she asks, handing me a paper towel.

"Better," I say.

I take the towel from her and wipe the dried puke and black lipstick off my face.

...

KIKI

I could actually murder Chase, and I swear I'm not prone to violence. There are six bunk beds in this hole of a room. There's a horrible faded burgundy rug that makes the floor look like it's stained with blood. The bedding is almost as dingy and used up as the drawn curtains.

"Yikes. Welcome to room 421," Chase says. He evaluates which bed looks the least likely to have bedbugs and throws his bag on a top bunk before taking a seat on a lower bunk, next to Emma's bags and gear. I make a mental note that he leaves the bed underneath his wide open, and I can't help but wonder if there's a certain psychic blondie he's hoping will choose to sleep there.

"What's that?" I ask, pointing to the top bunk nearest the window. There's a backpack and a small gray suitcase on it. The bed is unmade.

Chase glances over his shoulder. "That's someone else's stuff."

"A stranger?" I ask, my stranger danger kicking into full gear.

"It's one night," Chase says. I can tell he's suppressing an eye roll. "We're hardly gonna sleep."

I stand in the center of the room, feeling ready to scream curses at Chase—and I am not typically that foulmouthed, either. He unzips one of Emma's bags and pulls out his Canon Rebel. We use phones for B-roll and other stuff, but Chase mans this one for vlogging and shots he plans out ahead of time.

Money shots, he calls them, because he's a boy and he's still disgusting, even if he is the least disgusting of all the boys I've ever met.

"Just chill out and pick a bunk," he tells me. He motions to the other bunks, and I decide there are better ways to get revenge than cursing someone out.

"How 'bout this one?" I say, plopping down on the bed beneath the one he's chosen. Chase looks at me. I am definitely not the designated damsel for this bed. I cross my legs and grin at him knowingly.

"Sure, whatever makes you happy," he says. He doesn't mean it.

"You don't want to share a bunk with Chrissy?" I jab.

Emma and I have theories about Chase's feelings for Chrissy, and—hint, hint—we don't think those feelings are purely platonic or professional.

He fiddles with the settings on his camera and doesn't acknowledge my words, but his ears have a tinge of pink. His cheeks flame even in the darkness of this morbid hostel room.

I look around, groan dramatically and switch to the bottom bunk closest to the door, for a faster exit if any funny business should occur. I notice a stain on the bedding and hope to God it's not blood.

Yuck. This place is hideous.

I cross my arms and pout.

The door flies open and Chrissy enters wearing Emma's beanie. Emma shuffles in behind her. Chase shoots up from the bed and dashes over to Chrissy.

"Are you okay?" he asks, sounding way more concerned than he was about me. Still feeling pouty, I toss a knowing look at Emma, who rolls her eyes in agreement.

Emma flops down on the bed that has her bags, eyes scanning them like she's doing a check to make sure they're all there.

"I'm okay," Chrissy reassures Chase. "Apparently two hats are better than one."

Emma smirks, triumphant. "My skeptical mind dampens the vibes." She moves her bags toward the back of her bed and sprawls out, yawning.

"I'm scared to take my shoes off," I say, eyeing Emma, "let alone lie down."

"If we're going to be up all night, I'm gonna need a four-hour nap," Emma says, flipping onto her side. "Ghosts be damned."

"No way," I say, crossing my arms.

One of Emma's eyes pops open. "You're gonna be hurtin'."

"Fine," I huff. "You're right, I guess, but I hate it." I whirl around and unzip my backpack. "I brought us sleep masks and ear plugs." I pull out a handful of shrink-wrapped masks and individual packets of earplugs. I walk over to Emma first, splaying the masks out like cards to pick from.

She grins and chooses a mask printed with skulls. Chase chooses one with red and white stripes, then climbs up to his bunk and flops onto his back. I turn to see Chrissy standing near the bunk of our unknown roommate.

"Everything okay?" I say, nervous she's picking up bad juju from Mr. Stranger Danger. She turns and walks over to me.

"There's a book on his bed." Chrissy shrugs, grabbing the pink-cloud mask. "*In Cold Blood.*" She smiles. Yikes, morbid much? She takes the only empty bed, which is the one beneath Chase's, and lies down.

"I'm setting an alarm for four hours from now," Emma says. "Good?"

"Roger that," Chase replies, shoving his mask down over his eyes.

But I'm still standing in the middle of the room, freaking out. Emma glances at me. "Oh my God, if this is going to be a thing—" She scoots over, making room for me on her bed.

Thank God. I didn't wanna ask, but there's no way I'm sleeping alone.

AUGUST 10

i guess i'll sleep when i'm dead.

—E

5

CHRISSY

Even with Emma's extra beanie on my head I feel uneasy. After lying there with my eyes open under my mask, I rip it off and ball it up in my fist. The bunk above me has a wavy, discolored spot that looks like the result of water damage from the floor above. I stare at the spot, willing my body to settle down, but every inhale brings on a new shrieking horror.

The water stain morphs into a face contorted by pain and pure terror.

I squeeze the blanket, curling over onto my side and pulling the flimsy pillow over my head.

Even with my eyes closed, I see the glint of a knife with a long curved blade.

I try to suck in air, but nothing comes. Gasping, I yank the pillow from my head.

The knife presses against the skin of a pale neck, pricking the surface, blood spilling onto white hotel linens.

I grip my wrist, twist it in the sheets. Another scene—

A window slides open. Fingers clamp around the edge.

No! It's too much. I try to scream, but no noise escapes my mouth.

I shoot up in bed, yanking the beanie further over my head and ears. Chase stirs in his sleep, mumbling something low and indiscernible. He breathes out a small sigh.

I hear the metallic sound of a key unlocking our door, and I drop back down on the bed. How weird would it be to walk into a roomful of strangers sleeping and see one of them sitting up board straight and sweating? The handle turns and a streak of light from the hallway slices through the darkness.

I smell sunshine, which doesn't have a scent, but there's no other way to describe it. Warm, earthy, good. I hear static. Like a TV when the cable goes out and all you see is fuzz on the screen. I shoot up again, overcome by the quiet in my head. Peace like this is hard to come by. The static makes the rest of the noise dull to a soft hum.

My eyes land on a tall, lean male form. His hair is all rugged, tousled waves. He's wearing hiking boots and carrying a thermos, probably filled with water, since he looks like he was hiking. He's clearly a tourist who has probably checked out one of the famous trails in the area.

"G'day," he says, smiling. Straight teeth and an Australian accent. My heart skips a beat and not from fear. "Didn't mean to disturb." He walks further into the room and toward the bunk near the window. I notice a thin piece of leather tied around his wrist like a bracelet.

"I wasn't sleeping," I say, tracking his every move. Is he the reason for the static in my head? The only thing that has worked so far to block out spiritual noise is the beanie, and even then, it's not foolproof. I've never met a person whose presence silences the voices.

"Just needed to grab some cash," he says. "I was hiking Runyon Canyon. Now I'm famished."

My stomach growls at the mention of food, which makes sense, I guess, since I threw up its only contents after the elevator ride. He cuts his eyes over to me, his lips kicking up at the corners. I'm mortified when I realize it's in response to my stomach growling.

"Sorry," I say, still staring. I decide to do a little experiment, removing Emma's beanie but leaving mine on. Sweet relief.

"Do you want to join me?" the man asks. He's a stranger. I really shouldn't, it's against group rules. But if he leaves, he takes the soothing static with him. "I'm only going for pizza right down the block," he says.

The way he makes my head feel sets my nerves at ease, and I want to find out how he does that. It's still daylight, and like he said, we're not going far. And pizza sounds amazing. But—

"I'm Bram Kelly," he says. Sexy grin. "I don't bite."

No, I don't think he does. "That sounds great."

I scoot out from the bunk, standing up. He towers over me—probably at least six feet tall. I throw on my shoes and keep my beanie on, pocketing Emma's just in case. I do not want to have another meltdown on the elevator with this guy. I know there's no way to keep the psychic curse under wraps completely, but having an episode isn't the way I want to break it to him.

"I'm Chrissy," I say, smiling. He's got a curtain of dark lashes around his bright aqua eyes.

"Nice to meet you," he says. I follow him out of the room.

"What's the name of this pizza place?" I ask. "I wanna text it to my friends for when they wake up."

"Pizza Panic," he says. "It has a decent Tripadvisor rating." Every word out of his mouth is cute as hell. It's definitely the accent.

I'll shoot a text to the group chat soon. They probably have their phones on Do Not Disturb while they're napping, so there's no rush.

• • •

"Most of my mates decided to go to uni after year twelve," Bram says. He crumples the pizzeria napkin and drops it on his empty plate. "The odd few did the whole walkabout, gap-year nonsense."

"You didn't?" I ask, giving him the once-over, and not just because the view looks good from here. I should be able to discern more about him than just his raw magnetism without much effort. Impressions like what he wants and why. How he's feeling. Does he think the pizza is delicious? Is he as attracted to me as I am to him?

But right now, I have no idea, and it's magnificent.

"No," he says simply. I can tell by his expression that he doesn't want to talk about it. I don't care.

"Why not?" I pry.

"I don't usually talk about this on a first date," he says, frowning.

"This is not a date," I reply, but my cheeks feel warm.

"Then I guess that changes things." His eyes glint with

humor. He leans back in his chair, lifting his arms overhead and fitting his fingers together before tucking his hands behind his head. He's baiting me, trying to get me to press him further.

Now I'm annoyed that it's only static I hear and not his inner thoughts.

"You'll think I'm a nutter," he says. Drawing it out. "People always do."

"Try me."

He considers me for another beat, his aqua eyes slipping over my features. It feels like he's reading me. Prodding my armor, looking for weak spots.

"You can't laugh," he says.

I cross my heart.

He unhooks his hands and leans across the table. His elbows press against the plastic top, and he looks at me through his dark lashes. His expression is solemn, not even a little bit playful or jesting.

"When I was fourteen, my mum and I went out to the coast for a dip so I could practice on my board," he begins, the words sound like a brewing storm on the rocky waves of his voice. "I was still getting my legs to stay under me in the surf, but she'd never pass up a chance to take me out to the water, just us two. That day, though, this massive storm blew in, and we barely escaped the worst of it."

There's a flash of something in my head. Not his memory, just a feeling.

Pain like needles, everywhere.

"On the drive back, she took a turn too fast on the rain-slick road. We flipped. Over and over, I don't know how many times." He pauses, looks down at my hands, which are cupped together on top of the table. "It was days before I woke up. She never did."

She never did.

I know what it's like to lose someone you love and want more than anything for a chance to see them again. I never see her.

"It's hard to lose someone you love that much," I say, soft.

His eyes spark. There's an emotion in them I can't place.

Without thinking, I touch his hand. A jolt of electricity surges through my arm and I pull away, fast. His eyes flick to mine.

"You lost your mom too," he says, examining my face. "Cancer. When you were almost too little to remember."

"What the hell was that?" I ask him. I clutch my hand. It didn't hurt, but it felt weird. Like static electricity, but different.

"Sorry 'bout that," Bram says. He looks down at his hand and balls it up into a fist. He pulls it off the table and into his lap, obviously embarrassed.

"How'd you know about my mom?" I ask, mesmerized. Is this what I think it is?

He shakes his head and looks away. "Lucky guess."

"No, you touched my hand, something weird happened, and now you know about my mom. . . ." I trail off. He still won't meet my eyes.

Heat expands in my chest like a flame exposed to a gust of fresh air.

"Bram, are you psychic?" I barely breathe the words.

It's like I've shot him through the heart. He almost falls out of his chair.

When he speaks, he sounds breathless too. "Who asks that question?"

"I do. Because I'm psychic too."

Eyes lock. Time stops. A bomb could go off inside the restaurant and we wouldn't hear it. Whatever sparks passed between us when we touched are in the air now and crackling.

Bram's voice drops. "When I woke up from the coma, disoriented, alone, afraid, a nurse came into the room. She touched my hand and spoke to me." His eyes fill with tears. He tries to blink them away. "But I couldn't hear a word she said because, in a flash, I saw everything. My mum's entire life passed before my eyes, including her final moments. I knew life would never be the same."

I suck in a breath. I feel like an ass, forcing him to dig up his worst memory. I try to find words to console him, but unfortunately I'm better with the dead than I am the living.

"So, do you think I sound like a nutter?" His chuckle is strained.

I shake my head. "Does it work every time?"

"Mostly," he says.

"Can you try it on me?" I say. "Again?"

He looks at my hand.

"I'd need to touch you," he says. "Again. If you don't mind." Our eyes meet. I really don't mind, not at all. I open my hand, palm up, and he fits his around it. My hand is so pale and small inside his. The tips of his fingers are rough and calloused, probably from surfing. His fingers are long, trim and strong. He doesn't apply any pressure to my hand. He closes his eyes. I feel the subtle jolt of something, less obvious this time but still electric.

"You see the dead," he says, nodding. "You hear the living."

His eyes move from side to side beneath his lids. Finally, his lips break into a smile. "But you can't hear me."

His eyes open.

I heave a frustrated sigh.

"Ding, ding, ding," I say. "We have a winner."

He shrugs. "Does that make you nervous?"

"Yes," I say. "You make my head fuzzy. I can't get a read on you. But also, no. Because ever since you walked into the room . . ."

He squeezes my hand, which he hasn't let go of. I don't pull away.

"It's quiet," I say. I motion to my head.

"Relief," he says, because he gets it. I nod.

"I've never met someone like me," I tell him. "This is uncharted territory."

"For me too," he says.

"We're here for just one night, to do a reading of the hotel," I say. It's a letdown that I won't see this person after tomorrow. I hope we exchange numbers or emails, so we can keep in touch. "Why are you here?"

He smiles. "You first."

I tell him about the Ghost Gang and what it's like to be a psychic medium. For a guy who can see the past with a single touch, he's visibly intrigued by my accuracy and range of skills.

"I'm impressed," he says, resting his chin in his hands. He's a good listener.

"Oh, come on," I say, laughing and throwing a napkin at his face. He dodges it deftly. "Your turn."

"Well, I can't say too much, confidentiality and all that," he says, eyebrows dancing. "But I've been using my skills to get jobs with registered PIs to help fund my trip to the States. Easy money—they mostly have me looking into cheating spouses or crooked politicians, basic stuff."

"You're like a spy," I say, stars in my eyes.

"Sort of." He shrugs. "I signed an NDA, so swear on your life not to tell, and I'll let you in on a little secret."

I lean forward and hold out my pinky. He catches it with his.

He leans forward, almost whispering. "My current boss was hired by a very famous dead gal's family to do some reconnaissance on the hotel. Namely, the mother-and-son management duo."

Eileen.

"They think it wasn't an accident?" I try not to sound too eager.

"More like they need evidence for a civil case against the hotel"—he pauses—"for her *untimely demise.*"

My attention is tugged from him by the sudden appearance of a young woman dressed in a dirty soccer uniform, her knees all scraped up and bloodied. Her hair is a nest of tangles caked with sand, but we're nowhere near a beach, not this far into downtown LA. Her face is marred by a deep purple bruise and her knuckles are scratched. She drops into a chair, dazed.

I'm opening my mouth to ask if she needs help when her eyes shift to mine.

Cold. *Dead.*

Shot through with blood.

Another ghost.

There's the thin line of a bruise on her neck, made by rope or some kind of wire.

"Hey," Bram says softly, aware of my sudden mood change. "You okay?"

"Um . . ." I start to tell him what I see, but the waiter comes up to our table, blocking my view.

"Here's your check," the waiter says. "Whenever you're ready."

I blink, and she's gone.

"Let me get this, please." Bram grabs for the check. "You're the first friend I've made in America."

I look back to where the woman was sitting. She's vanished.

...

CHASE

Beep. Beep. Beep.

"Shut up," Emma says groggily. I hear her fumbling around for her phone to turn off the alarm.

"Oof." Kiki. "Watch your elbow."

I peel my mask off and roll over. After another couple of seconds, I force my eyes open. Since we passed out, it's gotten dark. The room is all shadows and creep factor. With some minor tweaks, this will be the best shooting location—

"Chrissy?" I shoot up, rubbing the sleep from my eyes. "Guys, is Chrissy down there?"

"Humans," Kiki corrects me, still half-asleep.

"This is a twin bed," Emma says. "There's barely enough room for two of us."

I feel around on the bed for my phone. *Do not disturb,* of course. I always do that when I'm napping or else I get a slew of notifications from YouTube. There's nothing from Chrissy, not a single text or missed call. I jump down from the bed and run one hand through my hair. The other I use to search for her number in my phone.

"You're panicking." Emma is exasperated.

"Where the hell is she?" This breaks the cardinal rule of on-location shoots. *Never go anywhere alone (buddy system!).*

All the buddies are here except Chrissy.

"She's probably in the bathroom," Emma suggests.

"We have rules for a reason," I say, "she knows that. Fans do weird shit when they meet their favorite YouTubers."

"We're popular, but we're not PewDiePie popular," Emma says. "Take a breath." But then her lips twist into a smirk. "Unless—"

"There's no 'unless,'" I cut her off.

"Whatever you say," Emma snorts.

Kiki is leaning against Emma, who has her phone open to the group chat. The light on both their faces makes them look demonic.

"She shouldn't have left without telling us," Kiki says. She sounds nervous. *Good, at least she'll be on my side.* I can already tell that Emma thinks this is just a big game. "What if something happened to her? Like she got up to pee and didn't take a buddy and—"

Great, now Kiki's freaking out too. She jolts up.

"What if someone snatched her?" she asks, her voice quaking.

"She's *fine*," Emma says again, glaring at me for working Kiki into a frenzy.

"You don't know that," I say. "We all saw what happened the second she stepped inside this hotel. The Hearst is scrambling her brains."

"So maybe she stepped outside for some fresh air." Emma shrugs, letting her phone drop onto her chest. "Or maybe she found herself a hot ghost boyfriend."

"I'm calling her." I swipe up on my phone and slam my finger down to dial Chrissy's number. It goes to voice mail. *Please don't leave a message after the beep.* I immediately redial. Voice mail again. "I'm going to go look for her."

Kiki stands up. "Let me get my shoes. I'll come with you."

"I guess I'll stay here and guard home base," Emma grumbles.

Then, just as I get my other sneaker on, there's a sound at the door. Someone is unlocking it. The handle twists. In walks Chrissy with someone who is tall, dark and handsome.

And he is most definitely *not* a ghost.

Back in the saddle again

i went on a date with a guy i met online. he was
nice and cute, but i told him his dead mom was
standing behind him and that was the end of that.
sigh. no boyfriend for me.

–E

6

EMMALINE

This guy is beguiling in a way that almost makes me understand—at least cognitively—girls who are attracted to guys. He's got broad shoulders that strain against his heather-gray T-shirt. Long, athletic muscles and wavy brown hair he keeps tucking behind his ears. It's unruly and wants its freedom, which seems fitting.

"Uh, hi," Chrissy says, eyes darting around. She's holding a boba tea, which is rude. The least she could have done is text the group to see if we wanted anything. Or to confirm her aliveness, but whatever.

Boba is life.

"What were you thinking? You could have jeopardized everything for—" Chase cuts himself off. I mean, if he ever wants Chrissy to glance even remotely his way in a romantic sense of the word, he is going to have to stop acting like her boss. "Boba?"

"Sorry, I was gonna text, but I forgot," she says, not sounding sorry in the slightest.

61

"It's not okay." Chase comes in with guns blazing.

Chrissy's eyes turn flinty and her jaw tightens.

"Not your stupid rules again," she says, giving him a full-body shrug. The display of her ambivalence is classic Chrissy. Call her out and she doubles down. Wound her, and her claws cut deep.

"We voted on the rules," Chase says, in his best impression of a hall monitor. I'm pretty sure this is the reason he will never, ever find a girlfriend. "You were there, remember? You agreed—we all did."

"Whoops." The chill in Chrissy's voice could turn water to ice. Without missing a beat, she turns to look at me and Kiki. "This is Bram Kelly." Her nostrils flare with annoyance. "Bram, this is Emma, Kiki and Chase."

She says his name last and I can tell it's on purpose.

"Cheers," Bram says. He waves. Australian accent. Well done, Chrissy! "I'm in that bunk over there." Then he lets his eyes settle on Chase. It's not a malicious or intimidating look. There's a sincere apology in it. "Sorry, mate, I woke her up when I came in. She sounded hungry."

"My stomach was growling," Chrissy says, giving Bram a quick smile. "You know, after I threw up everywhere." She scowls openly at Chase, who is not deterred.

"You could have woken me up," Chase says. *Ha.* Chase doesn't let on about his feelings for Chrissy, either because he's too scared that she'll reject him or too afraid romance will affect his ambitions for the Ghost Gang. In all this time, he's never once made a move or given her a reason not to date other guys.

"You all wanted to sleep," she says. "I couldn't." The subtext is fierce, just like her icy gaze. "I don't need you to babysit me."

"Sorry to interrupt, but, um, it was really lovely meeting you lot," Bram says. I glance at Kiki to see that, yep, she's got stars in her eyes. "Duty calls." He reaches out a hand and touches Chrissy's shoulder.

Okay, he's touching her. As a rule, Chrissy isn't someone you touch without her permission.

Chase looks ready to explode. I just wonder what business a traveling Aussie heartthrob could possibly have in Los Angeles that would take him out on the night before Halloween. Chrissy seems to already have the skinny on it.

"I'll shoot over a text when I'm heading back," he says, and then he actually has the guts to look at Chase. "I'd love to join in on some ghost hunting." He shows his teeth when he smiles.

When he's out the door, we all stand around in stunned silence.

"That was a dick move," Chrissy says to Chase.

"Jesus, Chrissy, you told him about the plan?" Chase asks. His neckline is turning red. I swear this guy is going to have a heart attack before his twenty-first birthday.

"He's here on a secret mission too. If he tells, I tell."

"We came here for the channel, not so you could hook up with some drifter." Chase throws his arms around in the air wildly. Oh boy. I suddenly feel like I'm in *Twilight*.

"He's not a drifter," Chrissy argues. "We aren't hooking up, not that there would be anything wrong with that."

"What does he even mean, *duty calls*?" Chase sidesteps the territory around Chrissy's dating life.

"How am I supposed to know?" she says, looking away from us. She's lying. I can tell.

"See? Drifter." Chase looks ready to commit murder.

"What's so wrong with being a drifter?" Chrissy fires back.

"He may or may not be a drifter, and either way that probably isn't a bad thing," Kiki jumps in. "But he is a *stranger*. You shouldn't have left the hotel, at dusk, alone, without telling us. This part of LA is dangerous." Chrissy narrows her eyes at Kiki, and I instinctively feel like I should use my body as a shield to protect Kiki. "And it's against the Ghost Code."

"Being inside this hotel is just as dangerous for me as it is out there." Chrissy points toward the window, her eyes filling with tears. She doesn't comment on breaking the code. "This isn't the Flamingo. The Hearst is alive, and I think it wants to hurt me. Look at what happened to Eileen. I'm scared something like that could happen to me too."

Kiki's eyes fill with empathetic tears, and she pulls Chrissy into her arms.

"We're not going to let anything bad happen to you," Chase says, but I can hear the worry in his voice.

"You don't know what the things inside this hotel are capable of." Chrissy's face is stone. "I do. So we're gonna do this my way."

Chase nods and Kiki releases Chrissy. We all look at each other. A tense silence stretches.

"Um, are you gonna finish that boba?" I ask. The bubble of tension pops. Chrissy groans, shoving the half-empty cup at me. Kiki exhales. Chase turns away and heads toward the bunk with all our gear.

Time to get ready to work.

■ ■ ■

The home base of our operation will be this room.

Even when we aren't here, we'll have a camera running at all times, in the corner near Chase's bunk. Kiki leaves to work her magic on a member of the hotel staff. If we're going to get into rooms that we aren't staying in, we need a master key for maximum movement.

I walk into the hallway. Despite the Halloween horror weekend downtown, it is deathly silent. I guess we're the only ones brave enough to stay here on an already haunted-as-hell night. I survey the setup of our shots near the elevator and outside the door. We will each have one camera on Chrissy as she exits and then we'll shift to B-roll.

I'd never tell Chase, lest it go right to his head, but he's taught me a ton about filmmaking, and I'm not mad about it.

There's a vestibule with an ice maker and vending machine halfway down the hall. I set up a small camera on top of the vending machine, out of sight from anyone passing by in the hallway or using the ice machine. I programmed it to rotate between thermal topography and normal video imaging, and it will run for up to twelve hours straight.

I set up another one right above the bathroom door. I hope to hell nobody notices it. These cameras would easily fetch a pretty penny at one of the pawnshops around here.

When I get back to the room, it's icy, despite the thaw I thought had settled in between Chase and Chrissy. Chrissy is holding her makeup bag and a fresh black shirt. She still has my beanie and hers doubled up on her head. Hopefully they're helping her manage the voices.

Chase is setting up the tripod for us to record our post-hunt interviews. He won't leave the camera here while we're exploring, but at the end of filming, we always rotate through confessionals about the experience. It's B-roll meets narration, even if Chase does direct the hell out of them. It's the part of the show that always gets the most comments and highest audience retention. YouTube fans love to feel connected to creators, and this one-on-one stuff does the trick.

"I need to redo my makeup," Chrissy says. She cuts a glare at Chase before walking out of our room. When we're alone, I decide to do something radical.

"What the hell are you doing?" I ask, grabbing a bag of chips and ripping it open.

"What does it look like I'm doing? I'm setting up for the shoot," he says.

"I mean with Chrissy." I pop a chip in my mouth and crunch down.

"The cardinal rule is cardinal because it's important. For safety. But I guess I overreacted." He turns and points to the lower bunk. "Sit down so I can check the headroom."

I flop onto the bunk and cross one ankle over my knee.

"You know, if you like her, you're not getting any younger."

"I'm sorry, what?" He's looking through the lens, so I can't see his face. His voice is impossible to read. No inflections or cracks.

"I mean, this is senior year," I say. "You might be running out of time."

"You're one to talk," Chase says. My mouth flies open in shock. I did *not* think he was that perceptive.

"Hold still," he says. When he looks up, our eyes meet and there's mutual understanding. This shit is not easy.

The door flies open. The curvaceous form of Kiki Lawrence is silhouetted, and my jaw is on the floor for an entirely different reason.

...

KIKI

"Whatever Kiki wants," I say, waving the master key around, "Kiki gets."

"You are amazing!" Chase's face lights up. I wish I knew what the tension was that I just stumbled into, but now that he and Emma both look pleased, I don't want to ask.

"Where's Chrissy?" I ask, glancing between them.

"Fixing her makeup for the shoot." Emma chomps on a chip and then peers into the bag. She balls it up and tosses it into the trash can.

I hand Chase the key.

"Some important intel I think you should know," I say. I need to touch up my lip gloss and check my eye makeup situation, but I'll relay this to them first. "The security guard is named Joe, and he's a nice man with a very substantial beer belly and three kids."

"Jeez, are you writing him a dating profile or something?" Emma asks.

I shove her. "He is also writing a screenplay set in a haunted hotel and therefore is not paying close attention to the security camera video feeds."

Chase's smile is immediate. "Nice, okay, so we can probably move around without anyone noticing."

"Exactly," I say, tapping my nose and pointing to Chase. I walk to my suitcase and pull out my sparkly purple makeup bag. "Now, dahlings, I need to get my face camera-ready."

I rush from the room, and down the hall even faster.

This place gives me the creeps. I know we're a gaggle of ghost hunters, but even for us, Hearst is a dark labyrinth of sadness and deterioration. I twist the handle of the bathroom door and walk in, immediately calling Chrissy's name.

"I'm over here," she says. When I come around the bank of mirrors, I can tell she's been hit with another wave of nausea.

"You don't look so good," I say, coming up beside her and placing my hand on her back.

Her eyes are dilated.

"Did you know someone was hanged right up there?" she asks, pointing at a protruding pipe behind me. "It burst from the weight of the body and hot water poured out, scalding the person as they lay dying."

I squeak and move away from the spot she's indicating, carrying my purple makeup bag to what I can only hope is a less haunted area of the bathroom.

Oh. God.

Help.

• • •

CHRISSY

I really need to brush my hair, but I don't want to take off my beanie shields until the absolute last second. Kiki moves my hair off my shoulders. She steps back to take a look at my ensemble.

"Give me a spin," she says. She claps her hands as I twirl once for her, and I can't help that feeling, soft and warm, sweet-smelling and safe. If Kiki were a color, she'd be yellow. If she were a dessert, she'd be cotton candy. "Lipstick?"

"I have some in our room. None of these are quite right." I look in the makeup bag and show her a variety of plums. "I'm feeling black tonight."

Her eyes twinkle.

She turns to the mirror and pulls out a compact, dabbing with precision.

Beside her stands a distorted dark silhouette sensing her every move. Faceless and formless, I feel its curiosity wash through it and into me until I'm racked with another wave of nausea. The smell of sulfur, rancid like rotten eggs, singes my nostrils.

The silhouette shifts, seeping dark inky water on the counter, but Kiki can't see it. She can't sense its interest in her. It tests the edges of her skin with its aura, reaching out with its murky energy to mingle with her bright light. I move around Kiki, right for it, while she examines her teeth in the mirror.

It stutters, watching me now, not her. It slides around me, an opaque mist that only I can see. Everywhere it touches me, my skin aches from the cold.

"Do you think Chase would let Bram join in on the hunt?" I ask, ignoring the spinning in my head. I swallow the swell of vomit in my throat.

It slips away, becoming one with the shadows in the corners of the bathroom.

Kiki shrugs as she pulls out a magenta lip gloss and un-screws the cap. "I think he could be useful."

"But Chase will definitely pitch another fit."

"He's not in charge tonight, remember?" she says. "You are."

"That won't stop him from freaking out."

"He was worried about you. We all were." She rolls her eyes and grins. "I mean, Emma wasn't worried, but no surprise there. I don't think even a dead body would bother her. She'd probably just scan it for electromagnetic fields and step over it on her way to get some Cheez-Its."

Her amusement beams like a glow stick.

Kiki doesn't know that there *is* something Emma has strong feelings about, and it's not haunting or tech-related. It's Kiki. But I won't be the one to spill Emma's secret. Kiki is the hardest to read when it comes to romantic inclinations. She tries on crushes like she tries on shoes.

And she loves going shoe shopping.

"But, like, if you want Bram to join, Chase can't stop you." She zips up her makeup bag and turns to face me. "Well, what do you think?"

"HD-ready, as ever."

We walk back to the room arm in arm.

This night won't be like any other night.

This hotel isn't like any other hotel.

The ghosts here aren't just the dead, they're the damned, and the darkness we've been trained to fear.

But hidden here is another mystery.

Bigger, beckoning, broken.

Lurking.

Emma is outside the hotel room, set up and ready to shoot. Kiki and I drop our things in the room. Kiki squeezes my hand, winks at me and walks out to join Emma in the hallway.

"You look amazing," Chase says. "Fearless."

It's just me and him in the room now.

Just me and him, the reason this whole thing got started in the first place. I would never tell him because his head is too big as it is, but Chase is the one person I want to impress. More than the fans, more than Emma and Kiki. More than myself, which is saying something. He's the audience I play to—my audience of one.

I smack my lips, spreading the black lipstick like ink across a blank page.

"Bring it on, Hearst."

Chase pulls the beanies from my head.

I step out into a hallway that screams with the deafening wails of a hundred voices.

Just your average everyday weirdo
FEBRUARY 18

i see things other people can't see. sometimes it
scares me. sometimes i feel special. mostly it's just
annoying.

—E

7

CHASE

Chrissy walks the length of the hallway, one hand outstretched. Her chipped black nail polish glints in the light, her fingertips brushing over the peeling gold damask wallpaper.

B-roll gold.

When she reaches the elevator, I cut. "Solid." Her lips curl into a self-possessed smirk. She can really turn it on, even in the worst circumstances.

"Ready?" Emma asks, poised behind the other camera.

She's wearing a utility belt weighted with her EMF reader, a thermometer and the Emma original Ghost Translator. Since Chrissy still has her beanie, she's switched to a backward baseball cap shoved over her long dirty-blond hair.

I walk back to stand in front of the elevator and hand the camera to Kiki, cracking my shoulders as I square them off. I'm praying to whatever force will listen that no one stumbles into this hallway before I get the intro speech out of the way.

I glance at Chrissy, who's watching me from just outside the shot, prepared to step in on my cue. For a second, our gazes lock, and I send her emotion that I hope she can read through all the noise in this place. Gratitude and amazement. The prickliness between us softens, like a cactus flower opening in the hot desert sun.

When her cheeks pink up, I know she got it.

"Ready," I say, swallowing hard. Emma presses the button on the camera.

"Rolling," she says, and then raises her free hand. "Action."

I clap to signal myself when I'm editing.

"We're standing in the hallway on the fourth floor of Hearst Hotel, and if you're watching this, then you probably already know the significance of our location." I turn my attention toward the elevator doors and press my hand on the ornate peacock engraved into the metal facing.

"Hearst's infamy dates back to the eighties, when the notorious Streetstalker lived here while carrying out a seven-month reign of terror that ended with his violent death."

Chrissy steps into the frame. The contrast of her pale skin and pale hair against the dingy wall and her black T-shirt is striking. I never storyboard shots, but we usually get lucky with the composition. Fortunately, Kiki has an eye for it, and right now she's manning the second camera. I can tell she's framed it to capture Chrissy's sharp angles and the shadows.

"When Eileen Warren checked into the Hearst, she wasn't anticipating the horror show that awaited her," Chrissy says, her voice raspy. "Eileen was born and raised by her single mother in upstate New York. She was bright, artistic, a promising writer."

"Those who followed her blog know Eileen was more than just a grad student with ambitions of being a journalist,"

I continue, picking up where Chrissy left off. "Under all that intelligence and drive was a secret inner world. Eileen could see things beyond this realm. And this caused her mom and her closest friends to question her mental health."

"Was Eileen psychic or was she a young woman on the brink of a mental collapse? That's what we hope to uncover tonight by retracing her steps during the days leading up to her disappearance and tragic death." Chrissy manages to get the whole sentence out, despite the sudden chill that has settled over this part of the hallway.

"Cut," Emma says. She looks between us. "Chilling AF."

Kiki grins as she hands me the camera. I'll shoot the three of them getting into the elevator and then both Emma and I will work the camera on the way up.

Emma puts the tripod in the room and slams the door. The walls rattle.

Kiki jumps back, nearly landing on the tops of my feet.

"Sorry." She shrugs, straightening up but not moving away from me. Kiki's fear is as predictable as the Vegas weather.

I look at Chrissy. "How's the head?"

"Loud, but manageable. At the moment."

"Want the beanie for the ride?" I ask her. She cuts me a look that could strip meat from bones.

"And get blasted in the comments?" She rolls her eyes.

"Are you guys sure we shouldn't have had dinner first?" Emma asks as she approaches, camera ready, face scrunched in annoyance. "Two packs of Cheetos is not really sustenance, ya know?"

"We'll break," I say. "We always break."

"I'm hungry now," she counters.

"The longer we stand here, the bigger the chances of us getting caught," Kiki says, eyes on both of the cameras. "What if Creepy Steve decides to do a check of our floor?"

"If we're going to keep jabbering, I will take the beanie," Chrissy says.

We are stalling and we all know it.

As if on cue, the four of us turn to face the elevator. After what happened on the way up, we're understandably nervous. Sure, it's great for the channel, but terrifying for us.

While ghosts don't usually interact physically with the living world, with Chrissy around all bets are off. We've been grabbed, scratched, pushed, bitten. Chrissy gets the worst of it. Emma explains it best: it's like they're using her energy to manipulate the material world. It's freaky as hell, and because we don't know the rules of the spirit realm, we never know what we're getting ourselves into.

Hence, the Ghost Code.

"Somebody press the damn button," Chrissy orders.

We huddle, like a coach is about to call out the play and we'll fall in line to execute it. Kiki grabs Emma's hand, tugging her close. I notice the tinge of red underneath the spray of freckles on the apples of Emma's cheeks. I waggle my brows at her, and her lips snarl.

"Okay, but this is the one time," Kiki groans. I raise the camera to capture her finger mashing down on the gold button. Her hot pink nails look almost alien in the dingy light.

We listen to the chime of the elevator rising. One . . . two . . . three . . .

Ding.

The metallic creak of the doors as they slide panel by panel to reveal the empty elevator makes every cell in my body shake.

Chrissy breathes long through her nostrils.

We step inside one at a time.

...

KIKI

As soon as the doors close, my breath catches in my throat. I yank the water bottle from my fanny pack and guzzle half of it, eyes closed.

"Jesus, Kiki." Emma is staring wide-eyed at me. I wipe water from my lips.

"My mouth is cotton," I say, defensive. "I'm nervous." Her eyes drop to my lips and then shift quickly over to the panel where fourteen little gold buttons shine.

She slams her finger into the one for floor fourteen with such ambivalence it's almost mean. Chrissy closes her eyes as soon the elevator lurches, moving up.

She lifts the camera. "Chase, explain the whole thirteenth-floor thing."

Chase slips easily into know-it-all mode.

"You'll notice in most hotels, there's no floor thirteen. That's because of a very real phobia. *Triskaidekaphobia*—fear of the number thirteen. Management tends to have trouble booking rooms on that floor, so many hotels did away with it altogether." He faces the camera straight on. *Professor Montgomery, reporting for duty.* "So here you'll see it skips a number, from twelve right to fourteen."

He motions to the panel with the lit-up *14,* no *13* in sight.

Chase's shrug for the camera is cryptic. "So if you're ever assigned floor fourteen, just know what floor you're really on."

The elevator jerks, and a sharp high-pitched screeching follows, and then we stop.

Chrissy's hand grips Chase's forearm. The lights flick off.

"Oh my God, oh my God," I wail.

"Chrissy, anything you can tell us?" Chase asks.

"I'm rolling in dark mode," Emma says.

"This isn't supernatural," Chrissy says. "As far as I can tell in the pitch-freaking-black."

My heart is a drum and my skin feels all hot and clammy. Chase yanks out his phone and turns on the flashlight. Chrissy has let go of his arm, but she's still standing close to him.

"No signal," he says, lifting his phone up to try to catch some service.

That's when it hits me.

"Blackouts," I say. Now I'm the one to grab Emma and squeeze. "Remember the front desk said something about rolling blackouts?"

"Great timing," Emma growls. She's still filming and now that Chase has his phone flashlight on, I can see her sharp gray-green eyes trained on me. They are wild and catlike. Kind of mesmerizing, really.

"How long do you think it will last?" Chrissy asks no one in particular. I decide not to mention that I'm ever so slightly claustrophobic. I suffer in silence, taking in deep breaths. Emma notices and wraps a comforting hand around my shoulder. It helps.

"Because of the heat wave, right? Can't be long," Chase says.

Chrissy's pale sky-blue eyes look menacing in this light. The dilated pupils tell me that despite her assertion that she's fine and this isn't supernatural, she's barely containing her sixth sense. This terror is bad, but it would be ten times worse if mixed with a malicious spiritual force.

A shiver climbs up my spine to the nape of my neck.

Just as the elevator temperature drops from sweltering to deep freeze, the lights blink back on.

The screech of the gears is the most beautiful sound in the world.

8

EMMALINE

It's a chilly ride the rest of the way to floor fourteen—which, sorry to be insensitive to sufferers of triskaidekaphobia, is really floor thirteen—but besides the teeth chattering from poor Kiki, nothing annoying happens. Paranormal or otherwise.

The doors open, and Creepy Steve stands there holding a black trash bag in one hand and smoothing his hair with the other.

Chase and I hide the cameras like the legit guerrilla film-makers we are. Kiki steps in for misdirection.

"Oh my God," she says, blinking, turning on the water-works right on cue. "Is this hotel even up to code?"

He looks startled at her accusatory tone.

"I'm sorry?" Steve's nearly invisible blond brows cinch in alarm.

"I should hope so," Kiki says. The rest of us slide out of the elevator on her other side as she holds the door open. "This rickety-ass elevator got stuck! With all of us in it!"

"I warned you about the blackouts," Steve says, giving his bow tie a perfunctory reposition. His features twitch.

"Aren't you supposed to have it on a backup generator so that people don't get stuck between floors?" Kiki continues, her tone shifting from annoyance to fierce reprimand.

"I believe we—"

"Just check it for us. Please. I'm claustrophobic AF and that scared the freaking crap out of me." I love that she can be as powerful and ferocious as she is syrupy sweet.

I throw a look at Chase and Chrissy. We're in collective awe of the wonder that is Kiki Lawrence, even though we've seen exhibitions of her magical powers innumerable times. It never gets old.

She presses her pink fingernails to Steve's shoulder, guiding him onto the elevator and pushing the Lobby button for him. She steps out and smiles, sending him off with a patronizing wave.

I wonder how long it will take him to realize what the hell just happened.

Hopefully long enough for us to give room 1413 a full Ghost Gang investigation.

Kiki spins on her heels, a giant grin splashed across her pretty face.

We honor her with a standing ovation.

"You never cease to amaze!" Chase marvels.

We turn to face the long hallway of floor fourteen, which effectively puts a wet blanket on our elation. This is a long-term-rental floor, and in complete shambles.

Time forgot it, and humanity doesn't give a shit.

Peeling warped wallpaper curls up to reveal cracked plaster. The maroon carpet is stained with bodily fluids of all kinds. Right where Kiki's designer shoe meets the roll in the rug is a substantial brown stain.

"Watch your step." I point.

Kiki jumps sideways, clinging to my T-shirt.

I turn back toward Chase and Chrissy, who are standing just outside the elevator doors. Chrissy pinches the bridge of her nose with two fingers. I start to film without orders from Chase. Chrissy isn't usually such a performer, but Hearst is bringing out the showgirl in her.

"Pass the camera to Kiki," Chase says. "You're up."

I don't like to admit it openly because enthusiasm is for dummies, but this part, my part, is my favorite part. Using tech to detect spiritual forces is hit or miss at best, and not nearly as reliable as what Chrissy does, but there's something satisfying about getting evidence to support our beliefs. Science that backs up superstition.

Plus, okay, gadgets are fun.

"I'll give a little more backstory on the Streetstalker and then we can cut to our slow crawl down the hallway," Chase directs. We're in a full-on freaking horror hotel and Chase is directing like we're in film class. Jesus.

Kiki flips her hair over one shoulder and grabs the camera. Chrissy tugs her phone from her back pocket, illuminating the screen with a tap. Bram the Stud Muffin hasn't checked in yet, I guess. Typical. Chase is watching Chrissy with open interest. She pockets the phone again without so much as a cursory shrug.

"Rolling." Kiki tries to sound professional but her voice quavers on the *g*. This is her least favorite idea. Talking about a serial killer where he lived and died is playing with an open flame.

"Floor fourteen is notorious for a lot of reasons—"

A door halfway down the hall opens, and out walks a

resident wearing boxers and a ratty fedora. Kiki lets the camera drop, her eyes wide in horror. The guy passes me first, giving me a nice view of his three-toothed grin.

"Pretty lady," he says to Kiki. She tries to smile and nearly succeeds.

If we're not careful, her bleeding heart will drain out all over Skid Row.

He gives Kiki the once-over and glances at our equipment, then presses the button for the lobby. We wait in excruciating silence as the elevator climbs back up. The doors screech open and he steps on. He watches us with detached interest as they close.

"Let's not be nice to creeps, Kee," I say, wishing I could chase that guy down to the lobby and rip him a new one.

Kiki nods, repositioning herself to start over. I pull the thermometer out to get some baseline readings while she talks.

"From the top," Chase says, and Kiki presses Record.

"Floor fourteen is notorious for many reasons," Chase starts again, and this time no one interrupts. "It houses the long-term residents of Hearst Hotel, and multiple true-crime shows have been shot here about the foul play that has occurred in these rooms. Many believe that all this violent activity can be linked back to an infamous killer who was once a guest at Hearst Hotel."

There are cold spots coming through on the thermometer. They look like little pockets of ice hardening in cylindrical forms all over the floor.

"In 1983, Walter Ritter moved into room 1413," Chrissy says. "When his room was raided at the end of his killing spree, police found a pentagram drawn in the center of the room in goat's blood."

I've just turned on the EMF reader when she drops that gory nugget. It slides all the way to red and then back.

"Kiki, hold the camera still," Chase says, his voice edgy. She's on the verge of a meltdown, and with valuable property in her jittery hands.

Chase carries on, stoic in the face of an angry killer's spirit. "Ritter was born in Germany and moved to the States when he was seven. A tragic twisted childhood led to a demented adolescence. When Ritter was seventeen, he found his first victim: a neighbor's Great Dane puppy."

The EMF reader shoots up, then back down. Kiki squeaks.

"During his seven-month stay at Hearst, Ritter killed at least sixteen women, all sex workers between the ages of eighteen and twenty-two. These were brutal, ritualistic murders, with most happening in and around downtown LA."

The needle flies into the red and stays there.

"Emma, *ohmyGod*," Kiki wails, dropping the camera to her side. Chase shoots forward, taking it with a firm grip and turning the lens on Kiki as she falls apart in a panic of pink designer duds. Her arms flail and her face contorts.

"Chrissy, come here," I say, mesmerized by what shows on the reader. The needle has never flown up and then stayed there. Never. Not in our two years of hunting the great unknown.

But Chrissy doesn't need tech to tell her what she can already see.

9

CHRISSY

Ritter wasn't a tall man. Or particularly good-looking. He had one quality that made him appealing and I don't think it followed him into the afterlife.

Charisma is something only the living can possess.

It's a flash, just a lean shadowy form there and then gone in front of a door down the yawning hallway. I'm thankful his face is a blur.

"He wants us to go inside," I say, eyes trained on the spot where he was just standing.

"N-n-nope, no, nope," Kiki stammers. " 'He'?" She moves close to Emma, her big brown eyes round and shiny with terror.

"You mean Ritter?" Chase asks, not even trying to hide his glee.

I point toward the door where I saw the shape. This is what we're here for. Eileen Warren's blog posts the week of her disappearance were erratic as she became increasingly paranoid, but they also contained clues that I recognize as coping mechanisms to try to ward off spirit attacks. She was taking migraine medicine prescribed by her doctor, along with a host of other medications that she described as "the cocktail" she took for her very real mental health conditions, conditions that can go hand in hand with psychic abilities.

In Eileen's three-week excursion on the West Coast, mentions of "the cocktail" grew infrequent, just as her poetic musings about life and the afterlife grew more pronounced.

Since floor fourteen is where many people believe Eileen Warren spent her last moments alive, it stands to reason that Walter Ritter might have had something to do with her death. We may not know all the rules of the spirit world, but one thing I do know is that ghosts affect psychic people in ways they don't affect others. Maybe Ritter didn't physically kill Eileen, but he could've gotten into her head and taken hold.

Tonight, if only for myself and the Ghost Gang subscribers, even if no one else believes me, I hope Hearst shows me something to help shut the door on this question for good.

"Come on," I say, weaving past my friends and walking to room 1413.

The 3 has been nailed on upside down and backward.

"Even the numbers are creepy." Emma is the first to join me; Kiki and Chase are hanging back. Chase probably to get a wide shot of all three of us, Kiki because she's seconds away from pissing herself.

I lift the camera for a close-up, shaky cam shot made famous by *The Blair Witch Project*, a technique that has been knocked off by everyone, including us, ever since. I get a good shot of the numbers on the door and then of the still-bonkers EMF reader in Emma's hand.

"Why would they do that?" Kiki asks, eyes on the room

number. "I mean, you don't think the number turned around by itself, do you?"

"Yeah, the numbers got so scared they leapt off the door and rearranged themselves all on their own," Emma scoffs, which gets her an elbow in the side from Kiki.

"You're up," Chase says, and we turn to see he's focused on our on-camera unicorn. The keeper of the skeleton key. Energy shoots from Kiki like sparks from a firework on the Fourth of July.

"Ready for my close-up," she says, but her voice quavers audibly. None of us reply. She's hamming it up. This is Kiki drama for the viewers as much as it is genuine gut-churning panic.

She unzips the fuzzy pink faux-fur fanny pack around her hips and pulls out an ornate silver key. Light touches its edges, and even in this dimly lit hallway, it sparkles.

Kiki blows a puff of air between her lips, her nostrils flaring. For a second she looks ready to hurl the key at the door and run in the opposite direction, all the way back to the safety of Chase's pool house in the distant Nevada desert. Emma lets her shoulder brush against Kiki's and they exchange a swift reassuring look.

Kiki slides the key in the lock, and it clicks into place.

Her eyelids close. I inhale a cleansing breath.

On the other side of that door is Ritter, or the demented residue of his murderous spirit.

They don't rent out this room anymore.

They don't let film crews in to investigate.

Kiki twists the handle and the door swings wide open. The air smells stale and musty, like untouched furniture and mold.

It's quiet and dark. Emma grabs a flashlight and hands it to me for future use. Kiki, who's trembling like she's experiencing a one-woman earthquake, takes the camera from me.

I enter first, blinking, as my eyes adjust to the dark.

As a rule, we never turn on the lights until we've gotten an initial read on the room from Emma's tech. It can screw with the results if we turn the lights on too soon.

We hear a click overhead and then a whir as the air-conditioning system turns on.

Kiki jolts, bumping Chase. He jostles me, his fingers splaying out over the small of my back. One finger touches the skin where my T-shirt rides up. A shiver shimmies up my back, and I can't tell if it's because of his touch or the chill in the room.

Chase's pupils are black orbs, but the light reflects in the sheen of them as he flicks his focus to where our skin touches. He yanks his hand away and tucks it into the loose waves of his black hair. I turn to face the entrance to the room, swallowing the lump that just formed in my throat.

We press inside. Emma has switched the EMF reader over to Chase's control and pulled out her thermometer to take a base reading of the room.

My heart pumps out a thrashing violent beat like death metal and electronica mixed together. It pushes blood past my eardrums in a deep ominous bass line.

The atmosphere is thick and hot, and once inside the room I can tell by the settled, dry pocket of unmoving air that the vents in the room have been shut.

"What's the temp in here?" Chase asks. I know he and Kiki have switched over to dark mode on the cameras, and he speaks carefully so as not to interfere with the vibe in the room.

"A wall of hot." Emma is on his left, her thermometer trained on the closet door, which hangs ominously open.

"Should we go in there?" Chase asks.

"Into the closet?" Kiki makes a tiny gagging noise. "Where he died?"

Ritter was found slumped in the closet, a bullet in his brain. His death was a coward's way out, eschewing responsibility for the crimes he'd committed and not at all reminiscent of the life he slowly, painfully drained from his victims by asphyxiation. When the police found him, they also found his victims' shoes, covered in his blood and meticulously lined up around him.

Trophies he couldn't bring with him to the afterlife.

I push further into the room. Chase is still focused on the closet, even with Kiki begging him to stop filming. I'm breathing through my mouth, because as soon as I rounded the corner from the doorway, I'm hit with the scent of bleach, sharp and pungent.

"It smells like my mom's bathroom," Emma exclaims. Her mom is a germophobe, and she takes it out on the bathrooms most days.

"Bleach," I say. "Why the hell would it . . ."

This room isn't used by guests.

This room is untouched and forgotten.

This room just awoke from a nightmare-filled sleep—

I sense eyes peer back from nowhere. A flash of teeth. A cackle.

But I'm the only one who hears it.

Who sees it.

I click the flashlight on and a beam of yellow light cuts through the dark, landing right on the dank maroon carpet.

A hand wearing a thin silver ring with an emerald in the center, its nails painted lime green, lies on the carpet palm up.

Unmoving.

Kiki screams and I jump back into the unyielding form of Chase Montgomery.

"You see her?" I ask.

"We all see her," he says. Our eyes lock as he takes my hand that's holding the flashlight and uses it to scan the length of the body.

A housekeeper, still wearing her uniform, including the apron. Her sneakers are dirty and her one leg is twisted at an odd angle.

Her eyes are open, unfocused, her gaze cold and fixed.

"Oh my God." Kiki rushes forward, hands outstretched. "Ma'am, miss—"

"I swear to God if you touch that corpse one becomes two," Emma growls. Frustrated, she motions her backward. "This is now a crime scene."

Kiki hops back, tears in her eyes, one hand covering her mouth.

"Okay, okay," Kiki whispers through her tears. She's dancing around like she's about to pee. That, or go into shock. "Oh my God. The poor woman. Shouldn't we check her for a pulse?"

"And risk leaving DNA on her body?" Emma argues. "Look at her—she is *really* dead."

"Chase, turn on the lights," I say, breathless. "We need a better look."

"No, no, I don't want a better look," Kiki says. "We should just get out of here and call the police."

Too late.

A light blinks on directly overhead, and even though the room is still dark, there's enough light to get the full picture.

Chase still has the camera in his hand, and it's still rolling. What the fuck.

"Turn it off," Kiki says, pointing at the camera. "That's so disrespectful. There's a *dead woman*."

Chase hesitates. For too long.

"What the hell, Chase?" Kiki screeches.

"That's messed up," Emma agrees.

"This isn't the time to panic," Chase says, finally pushing the shutter button on the camera to stop the recording.

"This is *exactly* the time to panic." Kiki's voice keeps rising. "I have seen this movie and I do not like the ending."

"I've seen a lot of true-crime shows. We have no motive and no murder weapon," Chase counters. "We're not going to jail."

"I wasn't talking about us going to jail," Kiki says. She looks at Emma. "Could we go to jail for this?" Emma shrugs. "Oh my God, I can't believe this is happening. We should never have come to this awful place."

Kiki starts in on another round of wailing. She crumples to the floor. Emma crouches next to her, trying her best to console Kiki's sensitive soul.

I crouch too and close my eyes.

Years of seeing dead people should have desensitized me to the sight of a corpse. But of course, it's not that simple.

I find my breath again, forcing my lungs to expand and contract, expand and contract.

I wonder about the woman's life, about her family. Did she have kids? A mom and a dad who will miss her at Christmas?

They left her here, broken, alone. This is the worst thing I've seen in the last two years hunting ghosts.

I open my eyes and let them settle on her name tag. *Anna.* Her head was positioned so that her hair fans out around her head like a sunburst, and I can tell from the crease in the shiny brunette strands that it was taken out of a ponytail or bun to do so. Her eyes are a warm brown with hints of gold and broken blood vessels in the whites. They look, unseeing, at the ceiling.

I want to close them, but I can't.

Ritter was here. I saw him, I felt him. He wanted us to come inside this room—did he know there was a body here? Did he somehow manage to kill Anna, even though he's dead?

God, that makes no sense. He's *dead.* Dead guys can't murder the living. At least not like this.

But what if it wasn't Ritter I saw outside the room? What if it wasn't his spirit that set off the EMF detector?

I hear a rustling in the corner of the room. Soft, lost.

I look toward the sound. Eyes, dead but still blinking, glare into mine.

The eyes stare and stare and then the mouth opens wide in a silent scream.

Gasping, the ghost's hands fly to her neck, tugging, scratching, wrestling with an invisible force in a silent deadly struggle. Her body jerks and she drops to the ground.

She twists and writhes and then—she's standing, staring. Blink, blink, blink.

Silent scream.

Gasp.

Tug, jerk, drop.

It will happen again and again until she finally understands.

Or maybe she never will, so she'll relive it, tethered to this place where her life ended so abruptly.

Trapped here, a resident of the Hearst forever.

I feel Chase's closeness even though he doesn't touch me.

"She's in the corner," I breathe. "She's reliving it."

Everyone goes quiet. The bickering stops. My eyes land on Chase. For one second, he lets me hear his thoughts. *We can solve this.*

I offer him the smallest nod of agreement.

We can't fix what happened to Anna, but we might be able to find the answer before the police arrive. The police, who will likely just sweep this under the rug as a drug-related crime and move on, like they did after Eileen's murder. Another dead nobody at Hearst Hotel. My heart breaks, thinking of this woman's gruesome death ignored and unavenged.

Now Chase and I just need to get Emma and Kiki on board.

Anna, whoever she was before this happened, died just like all the girls Ritter killed while he was alive and living in this room. The carpet may have been replaced and the room repainted, but that didn't get rid of the evil trapped within these walls.

I force the thought that follows to the back of my mind.

Ghosts can't strangle the living to death. This was the work of someone with a beating heart.

10

KIKI

Chrissy crouches and reaches out to touch Anna's upturned collar.

"Holy shit, what are you *doing*?" Emma throws up her hands. "Dead body of unknown origin. Do. Not. Touch." She shoots forward to grab Chrissy by the shoulder, but Chrissy bats Emma's hand away. She directs us with her heavily lined eyes to examine the girl's exposed neck.

"Ligature marks," Emma says, as she bends at the waist to peer at the purple and red marks streaked across the corpse's neck. Emma's eyes trail up to the ceiling as if looking for signs of whatever made the marks still hanging above the victim.

Of course, there's nothing.

OhmyGod.

I yank out my water bottle and guzzle. Dry mouth in the face of danger. Sometimes I really hate my body.

Chrissy is purposefully not looking at the corner where Anna's spirit is stuck in a death loop. How unbelievably awful for Anna to experience her death over and over with no escape. No matter how many times we hunt haunted locales, filming places famous for tragedy just to get YouTube likes never feels totally aboveboard.

We're shining a light on tragedy, and sure, sometimes that means we bring the living much-needed closure. Most of the time, though, it means we drag out pain from the past for people to watch with popcorn.

I'm gonna be sick.

"She couldn't have killed herself." Chase paces around the room, trying to supersleuth this horrible mystery. But when he reaches up to push his hair out of his face, I can see his hands shaking.

Oh no. My heart flip-flops and I feel woozy.

There is no way in hell I'm down to investigate a *murder.*

Ghost hunting is one thing. Dead girl in a haunted hotel room is a whole different game.

"We have to call the police," I say, adamant.

"If we call the police, that's it. They call our parents," Chase replies, and it's the first time he's actually let the camera drop. "Goodbye, Ghost Gang."

It's pretty low of him to bring that up at a time like this. It's also the cold hard truth.

"Jeez, Chase," Emma says. "Not everything is about YouTube!"

He waffles. My nerves are all riled up, my hands all clammy. I wet my lips, forcing the words to come out. "You can't actually be comparing our one-million-sub goal with a murder victim's right to justice." My voice is high, weird and shaky, but I don't care. "Because my best friend wouldn't do that. Not for subscribers, not for anything."

Chase's cheeks go crimson and he scrubs a hand over the nape of his neck. Chrissy stands up.

"Get out the Ghost Translator." She has a look on her face that is equal parts determination and rage. "We're not calling the cops just so they can screw up everything. Anna deserves better than a couple of LAPD detectives at the end of their shift." She blinks rapidly, the skin on her cheeks blotchy. I've never seen her look this close to coming unglued.

"She deserves better than a group of goofy teenage sleuths —" I start.

"Remember how the cops handled Eileen?" Chrissy fires back. I twist my hair around one finger until I almost cut off the circulation.

Emma presses her hands to her eyes. "This is different."

"Yes, you're right. It is," Chrissy says, her eyes on Anna's body, not on the corner. "Because we won't let her be like Eileen. She won't get stuck here; she won't be dismissed; they won't give up on finding out what really happened to her."

We all know Chrissy believes Eileen's death wasn't accidental. She wants there to be some other answer that isn't deeply, horribly sad for no reason.

"The police will do an investigation. They'll find her killer." I swig more water.

Chase steps up. He has a new confidence, visible in his squared shoulders and set jaw.

"And what if they don't?" His eyes tell a bigger story. A heavy one.

"Cases like this fall through the cracks all the time," Chrissy finishes for him.

The cops will go looking for reasons why the truth about Anna's killer doesn't matter. They'll let the trail go cold. They'll make it all her fault. Human garbage, a young woman with a minimum-wage job at a crappy hotel in the middle of Skid Row.

"This isn't about YouTube. In fact, if we screw this up it would mean putting the Ghost Gang on the chopping block and possibly being under house arrest for the rest of senior year," Chase continues, and it's impossible to argue with him about reality.

Chrissy and Emma might make it out of this without an extended grounding, but Chase and I won't be as lucky. My mom is already paranoid to the point of keeping me under lock and key at the first whiff of mischief, and Chase's dad is serious about controlling his son's every move just to maintain his own glossy image.

"Let's not waste our considerable skills," he finishes. I roll my eyes.

"Fine," I say, hooking my hands on my hips. "What's the pitch?"

Chase can't help the satisfied grin that cracks his features.

■ ■ ■

CHASE

"Anything else you want to share?" I lean in close to Chrissy, dropping my voice to a whisper. She bites her lip and shakes her head once. Her eyes close and for a split second she lets her body fall against mine. Shoulder to shoulder. Our arms graze. Her skin is cool; she always runs a little cooler than normal people.

"Ready, guys," Emma says. She pops her gum and raises the Ghost Translator into the air.

"People. Humans, y'all." Kiki swallows another gulp of water. Emma apologizes under her breath. She hates to be corrected, but, as Kiki likes to remind us all, too bad.

We decide to try to communicate with Anna. This soon after her death, Chrissy thinks we have a shot at more than just one-word replies.

When Chrissy does readings, she gets spiritual impressions. She senses truth and history, and even though the impressions are almost always accurate, we can't exactly take them to the police as evidence.

But we could take a video of the Ghost Translator telling us something tangible.

Hair color.

Height.

Distinguishing marks.

Whatever, anything.

I'm not going to lie, it wouldn't hurt the channel for us to help solve a murder. It might even convince our parents not to ground us for life.

A murder at the Hearst on Halloween weekend is even better.

I sound like such an asshole, but it's not like that, I swear. I'm not happy this young woman was killed and we stumbled across her body before anyone else could. I'm definitely not okay with the fact that she's dead. No amount of time watching True Crime Network could prepare a dude for the way eyes look up close when they're empty.

Emma turns around to face Chrissy. I raise the camera, training it on both of them and Kiki. Kiki is running camera beside Emma, but she refuses to stand anywhere near the body.

She's had two whole bottles of water, which means we'll have to get through this as fast as possible before she needs a pee break. *Ugh.* It's weird as hell to think of something as normal as pee breaks when a woman's lifeless body is lying on the ground right next to my Converse.

"Rolling," I say. Kiki nods, blinking a few times. Her eyes keep watering, and it's clearly not just because LA is almost as dry as Vegas.

Emma and Chrissy exchange a look of solemn camaraderie. *The skeptic and the psychic.* Our fans revel in their juxtaposition, but I like to think it's the genuine trust between them—between each of us—that helps set our team apart online.

There's a fast *click* as Emma presses the Ghost Translator's on-off switch to fire it up. The feedback rings and then crackles before falling into a quiet hum. We haven't had a ton of luck with this particular Emma original. Most of the time it just hums and screws up the shot when it feeds back in the camera mics. When it does pick up words through the static, it's always extremely satisfying.

"Anna," Chrissy says as she turns to face the corner of the room. Her eyes fix, and I notice a tremor of pain run across her face. The threadbare curtains, which are also moldy and faded, are drawn.

The edge of the curtain rustles on the floor like something nearby moved it.

Chrissy's eyes widen and dilate.

It wasn't a trick of the light.

"What the hell?" I breathe. *Blink.*

"Shhh," Emma orders.

I look up to see whether there's an air-conditioning vent

that might be open and causing the curtains to move. There isn't. I don't think this room is even air-conditioned. My eyes drop back to the curtain, daring it to move again.

"Anna, this is hard." Chrissy is talking again. Goose bumps rise on my arms. The temp just dropped about ten degrees. Shit.

I need to pull it together.

"This is hard for me." Chrissy moves and I follow. We're careful to step around the body as we go. "I know you're scared—" Chrissy's voice hitches.

I take two wide steps to get beside her, filming her in profile. She swallows, a hard sound in the deafening quiet. The purr of the Ghost Translator is the only other noise. Her eyes are wet, tears stuck in the corners. She blinks and one streaks down her cheek, paving a little trail through her makeup as it falls.

She doesn't wipe it away.

"I'm scared, too," she continues. Her lower lip wobbles. "Did you know I used to have nightmares? The same one, over and over. I was in a house with a long white hallway. There were doors at the end. White doors. And there was a room I wasn't supposed to go into—I was locked out. Everyone else was on the other side of that door. But not me. I was alone."

This isn't a nightmare. This is a true story from Chrissy's past. It was her grandmother's house, and the room was the one where her mother lay dying. We made it a Ghost Gang rule to never tell the spirits anything true about ourselves, especially Chrissy. Personal truth holds power. Power in the hands of a malicious spirit isn't safe.

I reach for Chrissy's wrist to try to warn her off this line of conversation.

It could be Anna listening, but it could be something sinister. And none of this is Ghost Gang protocol.

"I'm sorry," Emma says. Chrissy and I twist around to see Emma is reading from the Translator. Kiki squeaks out a tiny whine. Emma looks up, smiling. "Chrissy, keep talking."

I grab Chrissy's wrist and she shoots me a sharp glare.

"Be careful," I say, sending a thought to convey the rest. She shakes me off, eyes back on the corner.

"I've felt scared most of my life," she says. "Scared and alone. You feel alone right now, I know you do. I feel that, too."

"'Cold,'" Emma reads, her voice low and raspy. "'Alone.'"

"Stop reading it in that creepy voice." Kiki shivers.

"This is just my voice," Emma replies, and a half smirk curls up one corner of her mouth. Kiki stiffens her lips in warning.

"We want to help you, Anna." Chrissy ignores their bickering. "We want to help find the person who did this to you."

"What's she doing when you talk to her?" I ask. "Any change in her activity?" *Is she still reliving her death?* I don't say that part out loud.

Chrissy shakes her head. "Anna, I can help you, just tell me who did this to you."

I don't have a frame of reference for this exact scenario—*this is not the plan, never, ever the plan*—but I think Anna should have changed her behavior, even subtly, if she's communicating with Chrissy through the Translator.

Unless it isn't Anna at all.

"'Kill,'" Emma reads. Perfunctory, like she wasn't expecting that word to pop up. "'Kill . . .'"

"Emma, stop saying *kill*," Kiki says, dropping the still-running camera to her side as her body is racked with quakes of a building freak-out. "Please stop. Come on, can't we just call the cops?"

"'Kill,'" Emma says again, and this time her voice wavers.

"Kill," Chrissy repeats.

That word is being thrown around a lot in a room that already has one murder victim in it.

"You were killed. Who killed you, Anna?" Chrissy asks, slow and deliberate.

"'Not,'" Emma says, inhales. Her eyes are saucers. "'Anna.'"

"Who is it, then?" Kiki screeches, grabbing onto Emma. Their arms lock together like a vise. Kiki's eyes slam closed, but Emma's remain fixed on the Translator screen.

"'Kill,'" she reads. "'You.'"

In unison, all of our heads snap up. Eyes fix on each other.

"We need to get the hell out of here!" I yell. *Now.*

I need to talk to someone
NOVEMBER 23

yesterday i saw something that really scared me. i don't want to talk about it. i wish i could stop thinking about it.

–E

11

CHRISSY

That wasn't Anna.

That wasn't Anna.

I should have picked up on it. I should've known. She was trapped in the corner, reliving her death, hands at her own throat, fighting for air that will never come.

I should have known and I shouldn't have asked for help.

We burst into our room. It's untouched, all our gear just as we left it, and no sign that Bram has returned and neglected to text me. It's stupid to be thinking about a boy texting when all this is happening, but it wouldn't be the worst thing in the world to have another psychic around to help sort everything out.

"Call the police"—*hiccup*—"or I will." Kiki is still shaking, her eyes bugged out with panic, and now she's got the hiccups.

Chase holds his phone, looking ready to dial but also like he's formulating an argument despite Kiki's adamance. Emma sits on her bunk eating a travel-sized bag of Cheez-Its, watching their exchange with stoic detachment. Even with both beanies on my head, I can tell she's using the salty snack food as a coping mechanism for what just happened.

"We have to try again," Chase says, spinning the phone in his hand.

"We so"—*hiccup*—"don't." Kiki trembles. She dances from one leg to the other, places a hand on one hip and squints. Her pee dance is legendary, and I notice Emma's eyes crinkle with amusement before she flattens her smile and her expression goes neutral again.

"Hold on," Emma says, crushing the Cheez-It bag in her fist. "There might be a compromise here." They both look at her, their faces screwed up in annoyance and disbelief. "We have to call someone, that's clear. We'd be shit humans if we didn't."

"The worst"—*hiccup*—"garbage humans." Kiki shifts, tightening her thighs together. Her need to pee is reaching its threshold, but her need to call the cops is greater.

"Drink some water, Kiki," I say. "It helps."

"I'm literally"—*hiccup*—"about to pee myself. I can't."

Emma stands, commanding the room's attention again.

"Okay, but have any of you ever actually called the police before?" Emma looks at each one of us as we shake our heads dumbly. "We're a bunch of kids on what looks like an excursion to scare ourselves shitless and record it happening. We're a bunch of kids who lied and crossed state lines without our parents' permission."

"That sounds like an argument for why we *shouldn't* call the police," I say. Kiki's eyes plead with me. All the beanies in the world wouldn't be enough to keep Kiki Lawrence's thoughts away, and right now she's unwillingly reliving the discovery of Anna's body. She's desperate to make this right somehow.

"She was a housekeeper here," Emma says, her left brow hooking up. "Let's call management and tell them we were snooping around room 1413—blah, blah, apologies, whatever—and we heard someone screaming. We know the room is off-limits to residents and visitors, so we thought management should check it out."

Her words sink in slowly.

"What if they don't check?" Kiki asks, just as Chase says, "Genius."

"They'll check," Emma says.

Kiki looks at Chase, "I'll allow it"—*hiccup*—"but if they don't call the cops, we will."

"Deal," he says, nodding.

Emma is already calling the front desk. She exhales as Kiki continues to shuffle back and forth uncomfortably, trying to use her breathing to settle the air caught in her diaphragm. Her bodily discomfort taking a back seat to her desire to make sure they agree to check out our claim. Chase drops onto the bunk beside me, our knees momentarily knocking together. I can feel he wants to talk to me about what happened up there. About what I said to Anna—or whoever, *whatever*—it was.

"Hi there," Emma says, her voice bright and strong. She's not usually who we'd go to for interacting with the public, but Kiki is too freaked and full of pee to do the talking. "Yeah, this is one of the girls in room 421—we were on the elevator earlier, during the blackout."

She pauses to listen. "Yep, that's us." She rolls her eyes.

"Whatever. But while we were up there to see the . . .

view"—Emma clears her throat, trying not to say anything too revealing—"we heard someone screaming in room 1413." Pause. "No, we aren't high and we didn't scare ourselves with too many ghost stories, *Jesus Christ*—"

She stands up with the receiver in her hand. She's getting mad, and that won't help our cause. Kiki motions for her to calm down. Breathe in, breathe out.

It doesn't work.

"Look, pal, if you don't go up there to check it out, we'll be forced to call the cops and I can't imagine you want that." Then she adds, "And we'll leave a shit review on Tripadvisor."

That does the trick. Emma hangs up seconds later.

"He's checking it out," she says, with an exasperated sigh. She rubs her temples, and I wonder if she has a headache. The psychic force field of this hotel is strong enough to affect more than just me. And of course, there is that dead body we stumbled across. . . .

"You did it!" Kiki exclaims, and then hiccups again. "Good job, bathroom buddy." She grabs Emma by the sleeve, yanking her up and across the room. They fall out into the hall, clearly relieved. The door whispers closed, and now it's just Chase and me, side by side in the room where Eileen Warren once slept.

My eyes drift, taking in his profile. His nose has a strong swoop. His lips are plump and soft-looking. Sometimes, when he thinks none of us are watching, he applies a coat of Chap-Stick, the kind in the blue tube, to them. He has shapely black brows and enviable midnight-black lashes.

I thought he was cute the first time I saw him. I still do, even though now it's a lot easier to just think of him as Chase, business partner and best friend.

"We gonna talk about it?" he asks. I'm not sure what *it* he means, but my first guess is ghostly with a side of murder. I sigh and pull my phone from my pocket. I pretend to check the time, but really I'm making sure I didn't miss a text from Bram.

"Talk about what?" I set my phone aside and look Chase right in the eye.

...

CHASE

Her eyeliner has brown and gold mixed into the black. It makes the ice-cold blue of her eyes look unearthly. They pierce me and I have to look away, tug at the tongue of my sneaker and tuck in the laces.

"In the room, before," I start, struggling to locate the words in my brain.

I'm usually way better at communication. Like, I got a 780 on my verbal SAT.

"I didn't know it wasn't Anna," Chrissy says. She clearly thinks I'm here to interrogate her about why her Spidey-sense went wrong.

"No, that's not it," I say, making eye contact—as terrifying as that is. She lets me hold it. "The story you told Anna—or whoever—it was true." She doesn't break our connection. It's not a psychic thing right now. It's not her digging into my psyche, it's the other way around. I know her better than most people do. "That hallway, the closets, the room, all of that was from when your mom died."

Her lips drift closed. She doesn't have to say it, I already know.

I wonder what would happen if I reached out right now and took her hand.

But then her phone buzzes with a text she's not fast enough to hide. *Bram.* I've never despised a name more. The door bursts open, and Kiki and Emma come tromping in. Kiki beelines for the water stash, still hiccuping, while Emma stops briefly to stare at Chrissy and me with judgment.

"Bram's on his way back up," Chrissy says, not even trying to hide her elation.

"Wait, you didn't tell him about the body, did you?" I can't get the accusation out of my voice.

"Not yet." She stands, putting distance between us *and* the brief connection we just shared.

"Okay, maybe I'm wrong here," Emma says, steamrolling over our brewing argument. "But shouldn't Steve have called the cops by now? Where are the sirens?"

"If he even checked." I turn my attention back to Chrissy, mad as hell.

Kiki dials the front desk. She takes in a long breath and exhales. Her lips fall open in a wide smile, preparing for an Oscar-winning performance.

"Hi, can I talk to Steve?" she asks, sweet as pie. "This is Kiki, from room—"

The voice on the other end cuts her off, and without being able to actually hear, I can tell by the way Kiki's face falls that whatever the other person is saying isn't anything close to, "I discovered a dead housekeeper laid out on the floor in the precise location"—*this is conjecture on my part*—"where the

Streetstalker painted his pentagram in goat's blood. We've notified the necessary authorities—nothing to worry about. I'm sending up complimentary breakfast coupons to the neighboring Denny's to help alleviate your trauma."

Her hand drops to her side.

The sound of silence comes from the receiver still clutched in it.

"What happened?" Emma asks.

Chrissy and I exchange a look. Allies again momentarily. Kiki blinks, her eyes filling with tears.

"That was Linda," she says. "She told me to stop doing shrooms and leave them alone." She looks lost. "She said room 1413 is empty."

"What do you mean it's empty?" I narrow my eyes. "There was a body. We all saw a body, correct?" The others nod. "How can there not be a body there now?"

"I don't know, Chase, I'm just telling you what she said," Kiki snaps, and then shoves the phone at me. "You call back and give her the third degree if you want."

The door opens and the light of the hallway is snuffed out by Bram's imposing silhouette. He's got a sandwich in one hand and a backpack slung over his shoulder. The strap is too tight and it makes it hang awkwardly high, which accentuates his giant shoulder even more.

"Whoa, mates, you look like you just saw a ghost," he says. A smile cuts his face in half. "And it's not even midnight yet."

I don't mince words when I send Chrissy my thoughts through the psychic ether. *We're not telling him anything.* Her look is sharp, like shards of glass.

Emma and Kiki watch our standoff. The silence stretches uncomfortably, which I'm sure makes Bram suspicious about what he's stumbled into, but he does a good job of maintaining his nonchalant expression.

"Fuck it," Chrissy says, "we found something on floor fourteen."

"Something?" Bram questions, dropping his backpack near the door. The sandwich he keeps in his hand. Smart move. Emma is low-key eyeing it with envy.

Chrissy reaches out her hand, palm up.

"Go ahead," she says. What the hell? What is happening?

Bram's focus drops to her hand and he exhales. His eyes flick back up to hers as he steps into the room.

Long tan fingers curve around her small snowy ones.

"Not just floor fourteen. Room 1413." Bram's breath catches, and he adds, "A woman's dead body in room 1413."

...

My heart drops into my butt. He's psychic. This new development explains absolutely everything.

And yet, somehow, I hate him even more now.

He looks between all of us. Alarm works its way onto his face, along with nervousness and confusion, but he's also weirdly calm. Like this is just par for the course and he isn't at all surprised.

"I told you he's not just a drifter," Chrissy says, pleased as punch. She's being adversarial in a not-typically-Chrissy way. Not that Chrissy is never adversarial, but for as long as we've been working on the Ghost Gang, we've been aligned in our methods and our mission.

She's gone off book twice this trip—three times if you count this one.

Fine. I can play this game too.

I cut my glare at Bram. "Chrissy didn't mention you were psychic"—*convenient*—"and she also didn't mention where you were headed tonight."

Bram shoots a smile at Chrissy. "It was kind of a hush-hush thing," he says, and I realize his smile is a grateful one. She kept a secret for him. A dude she just met. *Internal eye roll.* "I do some freelance psychic work to pay my way. Mostly for PIs whose clients are suspicious spouses. But the job I'm on now is a little different."

"I'm all ears," I say. My arms are crossed.

"Ooh, you're investigating the hotel?" Emma spits it out, realization dawning on her quickly. Her interest has clearly been piqued.

"You could say that," Bram replies, bashful. "And that's really all I should say. But, honestly, this might pertain to whatever happened to you. I'm here looking into management."

"Steve and Linda," Emma groans. "They are *so* weird."

"This is about Eileen Warren, isn't it?" I ask, and even I'm struggling to keep my curiosity from getting the better of me. I still don't like Bram or trust him, or want him around, but . . . I feel eyes burning hot holes in the side of my face and I know the reason why is that Chrissy has turned her laser glare on me.

"Wait," Kiki chimes in. "You mean, someone thinks management was responsible for Eileen Warren's death?" Her eyes get big. "Y'all, Steve was on floor fourteen right before we arrived."

"Shit," Bram says. "Was there anything odd about his behavior?"

"He's a creep," Emma says with a shrug.

"I have reason to believe he's more than just a run-of-the-mill creep," Bram replies.

"And we're supposed to take your word on that," I scoff. "Without proof."

"Look, I don't want to get in the way of your whole dynamic here, but I think we could combine forces," he says. "Team up. Sort of like the Avengers."

"I thought we were calling the police," Kiki says. "Now what? We're *investigating*?"

"The body is gone," Emma says.

"Per Linda," Chrissy speaks up. She's been quiet this whole time, but apparently she's eager to jump in to agree with Bram.

"You think she's lying?" I examine her through narrowed eyes.

"I think it's possible."

"Because he's here investigating them, or *so he says*." Chrissy opens her mouth to argue, but I keep going. "Or because you have a feeling about it?"

"I'm not saying I have a feeling about it—yet. But I might, if I can get close enough to them."

"If they moved Anna's body, they can't have gone far," Emma says.

"*Moved the body.*" Kiki's voice quivers. "You say that so casually."

"We can't call the cops if there's no body." Emma is calm and cool in the face of Kiki's distress. "No body, no crime."

"Emma's right," Chrissy says, but she's still giving me a death glare. "We need to find out if Linda and Steve are as shady as they seem. We need to get close enough to get an impression." She pauses, looking at Bram when she says *we*. Gross. "And if Anna's body is really gone, we need to find her."

"You're suggesting we should look for a corpse in a haunted hotel," Kiki says, her breath hitching as she readies to fly into a panic attack.

Bram's eyes drop to her. "Put your head between your legs and breathe." His attention is enough to momentarily distract Kiki from everything but his stupid face. "It increases circulation to the brain. For panic attacks."

"Let's put it to a vote," Chrissy says. "That's the Ghost Gang way."

I don't say it, but I hope she feels it. It's ironic she wants to settle this democratically when she keeps going rogue.

"Okay, then," I say. "But *he* doesn't get a vote."

Hi

MAY 5

hi, still boyfriendless. bye.

–E

12

EMMALINE

Chase is outvoted even without Bram getting to cast a ballot. He clearly wanted to stew over it but didn't want to be left out of the plan configuration. He made sure the discussion was as uncomfortable as a physical exam, though.

We decide the top-priority items are: finding out if the body was moved and getting some psychic eyes on management.

Chase, Kiki and I will go back up to floor fourteen and Ritter's horror story of a former living space. Chrissy and Bram will head down to the lobby for Steve-and-Linda detail.

Chase tried to insert himself in the middle of the psychic duo, but he was quickly diverted by Kiki's refusal to go to floor fourteen without him. I was almost offended she didn't think I had the brute strength to defend her should a wild murderer appear.

I don't know what any of us will do if the culprit is actually incorporeal.

Chrissy didn't give Chase a chance to talk to her before she left with Bram, the Boy Wonder from Down Under.

Now we're standing at the end of the hallway on floor

fourteen. *Again.* Only this time, it's a lot harder to take the walk. Even if Anna's body is gone, we know it was there before. We know how ominously creepy it was to stand inside that room.

Kill. You. The memory makes my skin chill.

"Who's going first?" I ask. I lift the EMF detector and turn it on. Nothing happens. The place is free of electromagnetic frequency.

"Not it," Kiki says. We both look at Chase. He wets his lips and inhales. Kiki grabs him by the hand and squeezes.

"How about together?" he asks.

"Together," Kiki agrees, and then looks at me.

We don't take our time getting there once we start walking.

Outside the door of room 1413 the needle on the device moves up and falls back to hover in the green. Normal, nothing like before.

"It's quiet," I say, turning the detector so that they can both see. Chase's brows shoot together.

"We shouldn't have split up," he says.

"Why? Because you want Chrissy here to help us? Or because she's teamed up with the hot Aussie psychic."

Chase opens his mouth to verbally rip me a new asshole, but Kiki interrupts.

"Don't fight, please," she pleads. "We have a plan, and we need to follow the plan and get the heck off this cursed floor."

Chase lifts his camera and starts rolling. One million subs is still the goal, and he doesn't want to have a cliff-hanger he can't resolve later. Kiki puts the key in the lock and turns it. This time the click is ominous.

Turn around. Don't go in.

We are idiots.

The door swings open, and that sickening bleach smell stings my nostrils. Kiki turns on the flashlight right away this time, and we move fast past the closet and around the corner into the room.

"I can't look," Kiki says. She's got her forearm smashed over her eyes.

"You can. Because there's nothing to see," I grumble. I point the EMF detector at the corner by the window that Chrissy was fixated on. It's clear when I get close and nothing changes on the reader that Anna's ghost isn't here anymore.

Chase paces in a circle around the spot where the body was. He crouches, camera in hand as he examines the carpet.

"I can see divots where she was lying less than an hour ago." He narrates what he's thinking—for our viewers, I guess? I don't have the heart to break it to him, but this is *not* going on YouTube. Dead bodies feel like a pretty clear violation of community guidelines.

Whatever he needs to get through this.

I look at the corner, moving the curtain like disturbing the spot will somehow piss off the ghost again long enough to get a reading.

"Anna," I say, "if you're here, we would still really love to talk to you."

Worth a shot, even if it doesn't work.

When I turn back around, Chase is still crouched and looking at the carpet. It's dingy and dirty just like everything else in this hotel. My eyes track up and over to where Kiki is standing, flashlight shaking as she stares at the doors of the infamous closet.

"Kiki, hey," I say. She doesn't turn to look at me. "What's up?"

Chase finally stands, turning the camera on Kiki.

"Look," she croaks. Her voice sounds like it's stuck in the back of her throat. I cut my eyes over at Chase, who moves first. We came in so fast, we didn't look at the closet, inside it, around it, nothing.

"Is it her?" I ask, forcing one foot in front of the other. "Is it Anna?"

"Fuck," Chase says.

My heart seizes and my body slows down. It wants me to stop. Play dead, like prey; it's an evolutionary response to fear. I can't run away because I don't know where the threat is. I can't fight because the threat is invisible. But my brain knows there is a threat, and it wants to protect me from it.

It wants me to be safe.

I move slowly until the closet doors are in full view.

The needle flies up.

Written in jagged, serial killer scratches are the words:

Welcome to Hotel Hell
1313 1313 1313 1313 1313

The numbers repeat, over and over and over in a pattern—no. Not just *any* pattern.

A pentagram.

...

KIKI

A scream rips from my throat. Emma shoves her hand over my mouth to silence it.

"Is that blood?" Chase asks.

"It's not blood," Emma says, soothing and rational.

My pulse pounds, the sound of my own blood, loud and rhythmic, rushing past my eardrums. My chest heaves, sending hot breaths into Emma's hand cupped over my lips.

"To get that amount of blood you'd have to practically drain someone," Emma insists. I yank her hand from my face.

"Is that supposed to *help* right now?"

"Ritter used goat's blood," Chase interjects. His camera is still rolling. I shove him and his camera back. "Just saying, this could be an animal," he says, "it doesn't have to be human."

Emma rolls her eyes and touches the tip of her middle finger to one of the *13*s. It wipes off easily since it's still wet. She lifts her finger toward her face.

"Do not taste that." I grab her wrist. I get another eye roll.

She yanks her hand away and rubs her fingertips together. She lifts them to her nose. Her nostrils dance before she smiles.

"Smells like chocolate milk," she says. "Which makes sense because it's corn syrup. Probably from a film prop shop, maybe homemade. Corn syrup and cocoa." She licks her finger. "Delicious."

"That is seriously gross," I say. We all look at the closet door.

"Someone's messing with us," Emma says. "Whoever moved the body did this."

"Do you really think Steve could move a body and write this in the ten minutes it took you two to take a pee break?" Chase asks.

"Whoever it is, they are screwing with us, which means they knew we'd come back up to look," Emma says.

"They know we are here." I feel all the blood drain from my head. I decide to try Bram's head-between-the-legs trick.

"We don't know why Anna was murdered," Emma says. "But we *do* know that Bram was sent here to spy on management."

"So he says—"

"Okay, we know you're the founding member of the I Hate Bram fan club, Chase, but the only other person we saw on this floor—besides that one guy in boxers—was Steve. Not Bram." Emma has had it with Chase and his jealous act.

I know it's more than just jealousy, though.

Ghost Gang is Chase's baby. It means everything to him, and he wants to protect it.

He wants to protect us.

13

CHRISSY

I tug the beanie off my head and tuck it in the back pocket of my jeans. Under normal circumstances, when I'm not on camera for the Ghost Gang, it stays on at all times, but I need to be unencumbered to get a read on Steve and Mommy Dearest.

Especially if they're Anna's murderers.

I keep thinking about her face, her hands on her neck, that openmouthed silent scream.

Who could do something like that?

"You said Eileen's family hired your boss, right?" I ask, pushing the image of Anna away as far as I can. The fuzzy sound of Bram in my head is a calming soundtrack, like white noise when you can't sleep at night. He's sitting close enough that I can feel the heat pulsing off his skin.

He smells faintly of something sweet, like warm cookies that someone baked the day before.

The front desk is unattended, so we've stationed ourselves nearby on a dusty velvet sofa that has definitely seen better days. As far as murder stakeouts go, this one isn't half bad. At least not with the company I'm keeping.

"That's the story he gave me," Bram says, shrugging. He turns the bracelet on his wrist around a few times. "I didn't think much of it. Just another job, like all the others, nothing I couldn't suss out."

"So you didn't follow the Eileen Warren story?" I ask, mildly surprised. It made international headlines, especially once her blog blew up and people started picking it apart for clues. Bram shakes his head, and a few shaggy strands of rust-brown hair come loose from behind his ears. He tucks them back, and I notice that right near his hairline is a small, jagged white scar.

He notices me looking at the scar and reaches up to touch it with the tip of one finger.

"From the accident," he says, nibbling on his lower lip. "It's mad how something this small can change a person's whole life. Crack"—he snaps his fingers—"just like that."

I reach through the fuzzy haze in my brain that hovers like a cloud. I'm trying to see through to him. As nice as it is in the fog, I wish I could show him some comfort. I know how lonely it is hearing other people's thoughts.

"For what it's worth, I get it. It's lonely being this way," I say, and let my arm touch his. An electric current zaps, making the hairs on his arm stand on end. We both grin.

And that's the moment Linda decides to show up in the flesh.

She's tall for a woman, something I didn't notice when we were checking in. (I was too busy fighting the urge to blow chunks, I guess.) Her hair is bottle blond and set in waves that frizz at the ends. Her eyes are watery gray. She wears fuchsia lipstick, a smudge of which has marked up her chin.

Bram leans close to me. "What's our story?" he whispers, his lips touching my earlobe. He waggles his brows when I glance over. His lips are soft pink and kissable and, wow, I should not be thinking that at a time like this. You know, what with the dead body, killer management and malicious hotel spirits running amok.

"Indignant teen crying wolf," I say, pointing to myself. "Kind stranger just trying to get to the bottom of it." I touch his chest. (Oops.) I start to pull my hand away, but he holds on to it. When he stands up, he still doesn't let go, and neither do I.

We approach Linda, with Bram tugging me close to his side.

"Hope this is all right," he says, winking. "Kind stranger with ulterior romantic motives." I don't mind the contact, but I can't imagine he is crazy about it. I try to keep my thoughts super neutral, taking in my surroundings and not the way his hand feels curling around my waist.

I'm failing miserably at it, obviously.

Linda's eyes flick up, track from me to Bram, stay on Bram, and trail up and down the length of his body. Her lips quirk with unhidden interest. God, disgusting. She's like our dead mothers' ages.

I internally snort at my morbid joke.

"I hope you're not here about the body." Linda's eyebrow hooks up. *Hello to you, too.*

My lips curl in a grimace; hers turn down in a frown.

"Aye." Bram slides into play coolly, looking up at her through his dark curtain of lashes. "Sounds a bit wonky, we know, but hear us out."

She slides her eyes back to his face. Her interest pulses like an electronica beat—*oonse oonse oonse oonse*. Him, she gives a full-toothed grin.

There's a chip in the front canine.

Crash. Glass shatters behind her.

I blink, but Bram and Linda are unchanged. Chatting.

This is a vision.

I have to hold it together. This isn't normal, this isn't how it usually works—

Linda throws a glass plate against the wall. There's a man in front of her, hunched over and cowering. I only see him from behind, but he looks like he might be Steve. Linda waves an empty bag at him. The anger in her eyes is palpable.

"Hey!" Linda barks at me, bringing me back to the present. "I told you kids to stop with the shrooms."

Bram smiles. "My new friend here isn't high. She saw what she saw in room 1413, and I believe her."

"Like I said, no one has access to 1413." Linda cracks a knuckle on her right hand, her head bobbing. "So unless you kids want to pay for extra pillows, I suggest you go back to your rooms before I call security." She's definitely distressed, but there's something else. Something more.

Fear. Agitation. Malice.

This is my hotel, I hear her say, but her lips don't move.

A ringing, like an elevator emergency alarm screams in my ears.

A bellhop appears. *Ding.*

His clothing has been eaten through with age. His old-timey

125

hat is askew. His lips are straight lines sewn shut with needle and thread. Blood has seeped from the corners and dried in black stripes like a tattoo.

He cocks his head, looking right at me through narrowed cloudy gray eyes. It's a threat.

All at once, the ringing stops, giving me whiplash.

The bloody bellhop is gone.

"We run a tight ship here," Linda says. "Every day we have to deal with riffraff and Eileen Warren groupies who come just to cause trouble." She gives me a pointed look.

"Steve." I force myself to speak. "Are you sure we can't talk to him about this?"

She grinds her teeth until her jaw clicks.

"Steve works for me," she says. Her glare turns icy.

Frost gathers on the metal siding behind her.

The art deco sunburst carved surrounding the clock sheens over with condensation that freezes solid as it spreads.

The clock hanging above the desk cracks down the center.

I blink and the crack in the clock is gone. Linda and the hotel, filled with the spirits that haunt it, have a special bond. They don't like us questioning her.

"Isn't he your son?" I ask.

This woman is tethered to the life force of the hotel. She doesn't despise the ghosts and the darkness that haunt the halls. She loathes the living that come here to jeer and point fingers.

This one is just like the last, I hear her say.

Eileen. *The last* can only mean her. Did the ghosts at Hearst know Eileen was psychic like they know I am?

"Steve is a lot of things," Linda grunts. "On break is one of them."

I hear it in my head. *For her sake, I hope she leaves well enough alone.*

Linda turns to leave, and Bram reaches out and touches her wrist with two fingers. She stops short, and her eyes latch onto his fingers, course up the length of his arm and connect with his eyes.

"Thanks for your assistance." Bram's voice is smooth and soft, buttery and sensual and easy. It does the trick. Linda's smile is as eerie as ever.

"Enjoy your stay."

I grip the side of the desk, waiting for Linda to walk into the back before I let my knees come out from under me. Bram catches me, hands firm but light on my waist. He bends to make eye contact.

"Hat," I say, gulping air in to fight back the nausea rising in my throat. He tugs my beanie from my back pocket and places it gently on my head. I offer him a grateful smile.

"She had an argument with the housekeeper," he says. "I saw the name tag in my vision. Anna, right?"

"She's using the hotel as a front for some kind of criminal activity. I don't know what exactly, but I saw her screaming at Steve about more than just continental breakfasts and linen counts," I tell him. No wonder Steve is so curmudgeonly, what with the way his mother treats him. "If Anna found out what Linda and Steve were up to or challenged them in any way—" I cut myself off, looking up into Bram's ocean-tinged eyes. "Motive."

"Motive." He breathes the word.

"She mentioned Eileen . . ." I pause. "In her head. Maybe Eileen saw something too." I pull away from Bram and stand on my own two feet. "I don't know if you've read her blog, but I have. Every single post. And she was just like us. Eileen was psychic."

"The coroner's report said she suffered from delusions."

I grimace.

"I don't know about you, but they've been saying that about me since I was five years old."

There's a difference between psychotic episodes and psychic visions. Like me, Eileen had been seeing visions all her life, but unlike me, she hadn't found anyone who believed her.

I got lucky. Speaking of . . .

I turn and walk toward the elevators, yanking my phone from my back pocket. There's a slew of texts from the group and a missed call from Chase.

"The body wasn't there," I tell Bram. "But they found something else."

I show him the photo Emma sent me of a creepy ominous message painted on the closet doors.

"'Welcome to Hotel Hell,'" Bram reads. "That's gotta be the killer, right?"

I press the Up button.

"It's gotta be." The numbers on the old-fashioned floor dial light up as the elevator descends to the lobby. I breathe in a deep sigh and then blow it out. "Damn, Halloween at the Hearst. I think we got way more than we bargained for."

A haunting is what we came for, but this is so much worse than that.

The elevator doors slide open and Bram and I step inside.

He presses the number *4*. "I came here for an adventure,

some good surf, bit of that ol' American dream." He drops into an exaggerated twang when he says the last part.

I scrunch up my nose.

"Really? Getting hunted by a murderer wasn't on the bucket list?"

He chuckles and gives me a broad smile that tells me indeed it was not. I take in the perfect lines of his face, the swoop of his disheveled hair, the light gold tinge to his evenly tanned skin.

"Thanks for helping us," I say, letting my eyes drop to his lips.

"I'm helping *you*," he says. "And it's a pleasure." *Pleasure.* Those lips.

I bite my bottom lip. Now Bram is the one fixated. We're leaning in, heat building between us even as the fuzzy static sound turns up, volume high, my head full of buzzing—

The elevator lurches to a sudden and definite standstill. The light drops out and we're engulfed in a shroud of darkness. Instinctively I reach for Bram's hand to find he's searching for mine. Our fingers link, interlacing until our palms are flush and he can tug me closer.

"This happened before," I reassure him . . . and myself. "There are blackouts downtown."

"The heat," Bram adds. His breath pulses on my neck, and I'm turning, blinking, unseeing, but sensing him close enough to kiss.

Emergency lights, low and cool, flick on above us. The eerie glow touches the curves of Bram's face. It's a menacing light, but his face still looks angelic. His hand reaches up to cup my chin, his rough calloused palm pressing against my skin. His thumb brushes over my lower lip, the same one I was biting seconds before.

A drop of something wet splashes on my cheekbones.

Another.

Drip.

I blink and reach up to wipe my fingertips over the spot.

Drip, drip, drip, like rain.

I bring my hand away, dropping my eyes from Bram's to my fingers.

Blood is smeared over them.

Dripdripdripdrip

Up, up, up my eyes fly to the elevator ceiling.

Blood drips from long stringy strands of jet-black hair, splashing in heavy, iron-scented drops onto the walls, the floor, my face.

It's Eileen Warren, or what's left of her. Crushed up against the ceiling, her eyes wide and bulging. Her pale, pretty face is splattered with blood, distorted by a horrible openmouthed grimace.

It's a scream with no sound. And then . . .

A sound that is half human scream, half mechanical screech fills my head or the car, I can't tell which. I hold my ears and crumple to the floor.

I'm trembling all over.

"What are you seeing?" Bram demands.

The lights flicker. In the corner of the elevator stands a girl, white and frail and with stringy blond hair that's drenched. She wears a yellow-and-white polka-dot swimsuit and one pink sandal with a single, dangling broken strap. The whole car smells of the sea.

Her head shoots up, bloodshot eyes fixed on me. A deep purple indentation cuts into her throat.

She's showing me how she died.

Suffocated. Choked. Strangled.

Why are they always strangled?

My lips fall open.

A scream rips through me. Filling up space and time.

Hands on my back—I push them away. A voice, worried, hurried, panicked—

The sound sharpens. Now it's high-pitched, wild, manic.

My scream, their screams. It unhinges my ribs and rips my heart from my chest. It cuts me a thousand times all over, *slice, slice, slice,* my hands, my face, my neck—it burns, and I can't breathe.

Lurch screech.

Light chases away darkness. The elevator begins to move again.

"Chrissy." Bram's voice breaks through and I follow it back to earth.

To Los Angeles.

To Hearst, its ghosts and this cursed elevator shaft.

Poll time

DECEMBER 13

am i crazy? what if my brain is just making shit
up to mess with me? my mom took me to a doctor when i was 12 and he did a bunch of tests to
check for tumors and mental disorders. he said i
was fine, that i was just an eccentric kid, that i'd
grow out of this. i'm 25 and still feel completely
lost. maybe they missed something?

—E

14

KIKI

This level of fright is more than I signed on for when Chase asked me to join the Ghost Gang.

"Get me a Dew," Chase says, whipping his laptop from his bag and opening it on his lap. He's going to compare footage from the two shoots.

"You're really going to study videos of a dead girl?" I ask.

"Give me cash," Emma says, hand out and palm up.

"I have to," Chase says, rummaging in his pocket for his wallet. "I need to see what's still salvageable for this episode."

"You're not seriously still thinking of uploading this video?" I squeak. "A woman is *dead*."

"So?" he retorts.

"Oh boy. I'm out." Emma turns to leave for sodas.

"We can't just leave here with absolutely nothing to show for it. I've been planning this trip for *months*."

"Well, I'm not hanging around to watch," I say, grabbing the ice bucket. I follow Emma into the hallway. She waits for me as I tug the door closed.

"Hey," she says, her voice gentle. "He's scared shitless."

My brows knit together. "You sure he's not a psychopath?"

"Maybe a little of that too." Emma grins. "But Chase has *always* buried his feelings in the hustle and grind. I know he has high hopes for this episode to finally land us a big development deal."

"Pssh, hustle culture," I say. Cue my giant eye roll.

Emma chuckles. Her straight dirty-blond hair is shoved under a backward ball cap. She's wearing a faded gray tee tucked into her shorts, a flannel tied around her hips, and metallic silver–and-black Air Jordans that shine from the overhead light.

She spins around, walking backward to face me.

"I can't believe you're going to use the ice here," she says, grinning. "It's probably made with rat water."

I blink and then start laughing. "You're funny." Emma's brows shoot up. She spins away from me and picks up her pace.

Did she just blush? I run to catch up with her. *Am I blushing?*

The vestibule with the ice maker and soda machine is near the elevator and smells faintly of ammonia. Ick. I will never, ever remove my shoes and touch the carpet in this place with my bare feet. I do not need a foot fungus, *thank you very much.*

I walk into the vestibule to find Emma flattening bills against the edge of the machine.

"Chase wads up cash like it's trash," she groans.

I readjust the plastic liner inside the bucket while Emma tries to get one of Chase's ugly wrinkled bills into the slot, which keeps rejecting it.

I set the ice bucket on the metal grate and press the button. The ice maker whines and whirs. I release the button and cock my head, annoyed. It would be so like this place to not have a working ice maker on our floor. Or anywhere in the building. I press the button again and hold it down. *Scree-uh.*

"Damn, check to see if it's clogged," Emma says. The vending machine finally excepts Chase's fiver and she pushes the button for Mountain Dew.

"Ew, no." I notice a small metal latch on the side of the machine and it's open. Maybe that's the problem. I try to close it, but am met with immediate strong resistance. I slam the side of the machine with my fist and it makes a whirring sound that indicates ice is coming. I hold out the bucket eagerly.

I watch as ice pours into the bucket.

Blood-red ice.

I drop the bucket as a bloodcurdling scream rips from my throat.

•••

EMMALINE

Kiki's scream is deafening and I drop the soda can. She backs into me like a freight train, the heel of her white platform boot landing squarely and painfully on my toes. I wail and jump up and down, and she grabs me by the waist and tugs me to her. Her hands grasp frantically at my T-shirt, and I'm afraid she's going to rip it off my shoulders.

Kiki scrambles to get behind me, pressing up against my back, her breath heavy across the nape of my neck.

It's almost too much, until I realize I am being used as a human shield. Her hand flies out, finger pointed at the floor.

"What the hell?" I swallow.

Ice floods onto the floor, stained with fresh blood.

"Is that—" she starts.

"Yeah," I say, stepping closer. Kiki holds on, moving with me but clutching even tighter. "It's blood."

Before she can stop me, I heave open the door of the ice maker. A bluish sinewy arm falls out, narrowly missing my face.

"No, no, no, no, no." Kiki is quickly working herself into a panic attack. A killer is most definitely on the loose and now is *not* the time to lose all ability to reason.

"Head between your knees now!" I say, pushing her down.

"Who is that?" she asks.

"How am I supposed to know?" I can feel my chest tightening. What do we do? Two bodies in one day in one hotel? What are the odds that there's more than one killer?

No, the odds are much better that a serial killer is on the loose. Inside the hotel. Where we are staying.

I'm gonna hurl.

The ice maker starts to buzz, ready with fresh ice. I hear the ice raining down with a sickening *splat* on the dead person inside the machine. The force of the avalanche of ice causes the body to shift.

I yelp and leap back.

Bloodstained ice cascades to the ground.

A man in uniform, openmouthed, dead-eyed, his throat slit from ear to ear, drops down.

It's Steve.

Kiki raises her head from between her knees and collapses. So much for avoiding a panic attack. She's shaking with tears, her trembling hands covering her face.

All I can do is stare and stare and stare.

I've never seen this much blood.

The ice cubes that have collected on the gray tile floor melt into bloody puddles.

I pull my phone from my pocket with a shaky hand and dial Chase.

It rings once. "What's taking so lo—"

"Get down here," I say. My voice is cold. "Now."

I hang up and listen for the sound of our room door opening and closing. Listen for Chase's footsteps.

Kiki is a puddle on the floor. She stares at Steve's body, her pretty face contorted with terror.

"I just talked to him like an hour ago," she says, her voice numb, her eyes wide and glassy. "This happened because we found Anna. This happened because of us."

"This happened because of some demented killer," I say, shaking my head. Kiki looks up into my eyes, her cheeks streaked with tears. I don't think, I just bend down and tug her into a hug. "This isn't our fault."

Her lashes flutter against my neck.

"Guess we can eliminate Steve as a suspect," Chase says, an inappropriate amount of lightness edging through his voice. I let Kiki go and turn to glower at him.

All the color has drained from his face.

Finding one dead body is messed up. One dead body is enough to give you nightmares for life.

Two is the kind of thing that leads to PTSD and a lifetime of therapy.

Chase, don't slip on me now.

"What are you thinking?" I ask. Years of watching *Criminal Minds* and *Crime Scene Investigation* with his mom have trained Chase to scrutinize the details around him. That might help snap him out of his momentary stupor.

He blinks a few times, regaining his composure, and looks around the scene with sharp eyes. He moves further into the tiny vestibule.

"I think"—he examines the crime scene, tilting his head side to side as he tries to get a good look inside the ice maker—"his throat was slashed inside that thing. There's too much blood in there and not enough out here for it to be a kill, drag and drop."

Kiki makes a gagging noise and holds her stomach.

Chase bends down, getting as close as he can to Steve without touching him. The ice is still melting, turning the tiles slick with water and blood. Kiki is still shivering against the wall, but at least she's stopped crying.

"Chase, what are you doing?" I ask.

"Someone hit him over the head from behind," he says, motioning to the bloody matted lump on the back of Steve's greasy head. "Killed him while he was unconscious probably."

"How nice of them," Kiki says, clutching her stomach.

The *ding* of the elevator doors opening sings through the hallway.

"Fuck, we have to hide him," I say, rushing forward and pushing Steve's body back up into the ice machine. It doesn't count as touching the body if it's just my shoe. (Please let there be no blood on my shoe.)

"You've got to be kidding me," Chase spits.

"What are you doing?" Kiki whisper-screams.

"Block the entry, Kee," I plead.

Kiki makes a noise that sounds more like a wounded puppy

than a human being before trying to position herself in the doorway to take up as much space as possible.

"This is legit tampering with a crime scene," Chase says.

"The damage is done," I growl. He's just standing there, shell-shocked and stiff as a board. I snap my fingers in front of his face. *"Help me."*

"There's bloody ice everywhere," he says, trying not to soil his Converse. We're all gonna need new shoes after this trip to hell.

"Kick it under the machine?" I'm not super clear on the best way to hide a murder from a tourist walking off the elevator at two a.m.

"Maybe they'll be too tired to notice," Chase says. "I'm not getting blood on my shoes."

"Better your Converse than my Jordans." I leverage my shoulder against the ice maker door and grunt.

"What is going on?" Chrissy's voice cuts through our bickering. I turn to see her and Bram rushing into the room. It's getting crowded in here.

Chrissy has both beanies on her head. She looks exhausted and shaken—but we all look like that right now. She's standing awfully close to Bram. Good for her, getting some, except for, ya know, it happening in conjunction with all this murder and gruesomeness.

"Are you lot destroying evidence?" Bram asks, eyes wide with shock.

"No, we're not *destroying evidence*," Chase replies, mocking Bram's accent.

"Is that your impression of me?" Bram's laugh is full-bodied.

Chase glares at him, and I'm glad he doesn't have access to

139

anything sharp, or else there'd be a third corpse to deal with tonight. He shoots up straight, letting the door of the ice maker slide open a little. I grunt, trying to hold it in place by myself.

"Steve is dead," Chrissy says, cutting through the tension.

"Can you see his spirit?" Bram asks.

"No." Chrissy shakes her head. "If he's around, he's not showing himself to me. But I read it in them."

"Okay, I hate to say it," I interject. *Really, really hate it.* "We can't leave him in the ice machine for randos to find and report." I grit my teeth. If we found him this way, anyone else can too.

"No way, we are not moving the body." Kiki has joined us. I point to the doorway. She rolls her eyes and returns to her position as lookout.

"Flip you," Bram says to Chase. "Heads or tails." He doesn't pull out a coin, because he's joking. Chase has never looked more bloodthirsty in his life.

"Everyone, take a limb."

Jerry
OCTOBER 30

one of my new coworkers is a dead guy. he was
shot in the face during an armed robbery. imagine
spending your afterlife in a fried chicken joint. no
thank you.

—E

15

CHASE

We situate Steve in the bathroom shower stall and close the curtain. It's gruesome and I don't want to talk about it, but let's just say that after hoisting him from the ice, carrying him down the hall and cleaning up the bloody evidence, we all had to scrub our hands, arms and brains and change clothes.

One by one.

Kiki managed to snag an Out of Order sign from a maintenance closet, since she refused to touch the body, and hung it on the shower curtain to discourage anyone from looking inside. It might not work long term, but it should at least buy us some time.

And this way we don't have the body stashed in our room because *ick.*

God, and after all this, I have an AP physics exam on Monday. Which I haven't studied for. Oops.

"What's our next move?" Kiki asks, sitting next to Emma on the bunk. "Now that we have *moved a dead body* and could easily be prime suspects in a *murder.*"

At least she's stopped insisting we call the police. We're in too deep now, and we all know it.

We don't know much else, though, and if we don't get some answers plus proof, this will have to remain our little secret or else we'll not only be grounded but possibly also cuffed and interrogated.

"Hearst is home to malicious spirits plus some kind of dark criminal activity," Chrissy says, followed by a deep, tired sigh. We have all lived a thousand lifetimes in less than twenty-four hours.

She gives us the rundown about her little tête-à-tête with Linda, and if it's all true and actually playing out the way Chrissy thinks it is, there's no telling how far Linda will go to keep her racket under wraps. Including offing her own son.

Linda might have cop friends. She might have cops in her pocket.

That sort of shit happens in LA all the time. At least it does on TV.

We gotta get proof on camera.

Plus, *on camera* means *on YouTube,* and there's no way this doesn't blow up on the channel. It will be juicy and controversial and terrifying. Just what the internet loves the most.

One million subs is still attainable. My plan isn't totally shot to hell yet.

Despite the Bram in the room. He tucks the front hem of his fresh black T-shirt into his jeans. He looks like a Calvin Klein underwear model. I hate him.

"Wait, do we still think Racketeer Linda and Creepy Steve killed Anna? After we found Steve dead in the ice machine?" Emma asks, shoving three Cheetos in her mouth at the same time and chomping down. Despite the steady intake of junk food, she's still developing an edge of hangry about her. Going out for real food isn't an option, but Emma on an empty tank isn't much better than murderers running loose, in my humble opinion.

"How can you eat at a time like this?" Kiki is visibly shocked. She's on her fourth bottle of room-temp Smartwater and moments away from needing another pee break.

"I would murder a burger right now," Emma replies.

"Don't say that word." Kiki gulps more water. *"Please."*

Emma shoots to her feet. "The cameras."

"Cameras?" Bram's eyes narrow in confusion. *Some psychic.*

"We set up hidden cameras on this floor," Emma explains, dropping the bag of Cheetos on the bunk. "There is no way they didn't catch something useful."

Emma runs to the door in a flurry and yanks it open with adrenaline-fueled force. It slams against the wall, hard. We watch the hallway, dazed by her sudden exit.

"Fuck!" Emma yells from the hall, bolting past our room in the direction of the bathroom.

She reappears in the doorway, breathless, her hands on her knees.

"Gone," she says, gasping. She is definitely not an athlete. She walks into the room and slams the door behind her, rattling the hinges. "All. Gone. Damn it!"

"Dude, calm down," I say, annoyed. "We get it. The cameras are gone."

"Six hundred bucks, Chase. Gone."

"We can replace the cameras," I reply. She crosses her arms over her chest. "The footage is what matters right now."

"I didn't set it to upload to the cloud," Emma says, pushing back her hair from her face.

"That was smart," I say, an edge in my own voice.

Her death glare would scare a ghost. "The network wasn't secure, douchebag. I didn't want to get gutted."

"So it didn't back up? Like at all?" I'm dumbfounded. We always back up camera feeds to the cloud.

"Not a single freaking second."

"We need a plan B."

This is sort of our thing. When shit goes wrong, which it usually does, the Ghost Gang kicks into problem-solving mode. We play idea spitball.

That is, when there's not an Aussie superdouche in our midst.

Bram sheepishly raises one hand. Chrissy's cheeks get pink. She probably thinks it's adorable that he's helping us. Gag.

"My boss might have some intel for us," Bram says, without being called on. "If you want, I can check in with him. Could be useful if we're looking for motive."

Chrissy smiles in response. "I think that's a solid idea."

I think that's a solid idea. Barf.

"Ace," he replies. "I'll just step out to give him a call." He pulls his phone out of his pocket as he leaves the room.

"We don't have footage, but maybe—" Emma starts.

"I think he's lying," I interrupt her as soon as the door shuts behind Bram. Chrissy's eyes shoot to mine without missing a beat.

"What are you talking about?" She glares at me. I reach into my back pocket.

"I went through his backpack right before Steve on Ice."

"You went through his stuff?" Chrissy's face turns red with anger.

"When you were supposed to be going over footage?" Kiki sits up.

"I took my chance, guys—"

"Humans, damn it," Kiki says, lips tight.

"We have to trust him a helluva lot to believe his story without any proof."

"Chrissy would know," Emma starts, "if he wasn't telling the truth. Right, Chrissy?"

Chrissy is silent. Her eyes burn a hole through me. I can feel the heat.

"Chrissy said it herself. He makes her head fuzzy." I look at her, raising my eyebrows. "You don't know what he's thinking, do you?"

She clenches her jaw and shakes her head once.

"His name isn't Bram Kelly," I say.

I try to hand her the passport I lifted from his backpack. At first, she doesn't want to take it or remove her glare from my face. I flip the passport open and raise it up in front of her face. Reluctantly, she slides her gaze to it.

"Roy Walker," I say.

"And?" She snatches the passport from me.

"He lied about his name. What else is he lying about?"

"How do you know he's lying?" She lifts one eyebrow. "How do you know this isn't a fake to protect his identity? Or maybe he just wanted to go by a different name and start over."

My mouth drops open. I'm alarmed that she's this quick to dismiss Bram's lie.

"You don't know anything, but you do *know* you want it to be something nefarious," she says.

"No, I want you to consider that this dude isn't telling you the whole truth."

She cocks one hip, laughing. "And you are?"

"What's that supposed to mean?"

"Danger, danger," Emma says, waving her hands. But Chrissy's on the warpath. And it's too late for me to surrender.

"You're just looking for an excuse to throw suspicion on him because you're jealous."

The words fire from her lips like flaming darts.

"I'm not jealous, I'm just worried about you." It's mostly true.

"You won't even give Bram a chance. Finally, I meet someone who's just like me. Who makes me feel less alone, less isolated, less like a freak."

The room is stone-cold silent. I look at Kiki, then Emma; they look at me. We're all shocked by this admission.

"We had no idea you felt that way, Chrissy," Kiki says, reaching out to touch Chrissy's hand. Chrissy pulls away from Kiki like her hand is red hot.

"And now all you want to do is make judgments about Bram that he doesn't deserve. Because of a freaking passport." She waves the passport around.

"I can't help it if I don't trust him," I say, trying to reason with her.

"And what about you, Chase? You drag us to this horrible hotel that scrambles my brain. You talk nonstop about one million subscribers and that stupid Gold Play Button. You don't even stop recording when we find a dead body." Chrissy crosses her arms over her chest defiantly. "I'm starting to think *you're* the one we shouldn't trust."

I can't believe I'm hearing this from her, after everything. I was the first one to believe her about her psychic abilities. I was the one who introduced her to Kiki and Emma. And sure, I'm the one who's never told her about my crush, who never likes it when she dates other guys because they aren't me, and it's my own fault for thinking I had all the time in the world.

"You don't really mean that, Chrissy," Kiki says, tears filling her eyes.

"Chase is our best friend," Emma adds, coming to my defense.

Chrissy shrugs off the emotion I can tell she feels from the sheen of moisture in her eyes. "I don't know what to believe anymore."

"He's in your head," I say. I look at the floor, unwilling to meet her gaze any longer. "I don't know if we can trust *you* with him around."

"You had *two years*," she says. The words are laced with venom.

Like it was just that easy.

Like she didn't intimidate the hell out of me. Like we didn't have to get the channel off the ground for all our sakes. Like I didn't want to tell her all the time but was terrified of ruining the friendship. Of jeopardizing everything we'd built together.

"Okay, this is way too intense after slashed-throat Steve and strangled Anna," Emma says, raising her hands in defeat. "You kids sort this out amongst yourselves, I'm gonna go look for our cameras."

She spins on her heels and exits the room, leaving the door wide open.

"Emma, where are you going?" Kiki's gaze flies from the exit back to me and Chrissy. "What about the Ghost Code?"

"Screw the Ghost Code!" Emma shouts.

I roll my eyes. Kiki stiffens her lips and stalks out of the room.

When I look back at Chrissy, she's shut the passport. Without a word she walks over to Bram's backpack and stows it back inside.

I take a step toward her and she puts a hand up to stop me from coming any closer.

"Don't. And don't follow me."

She walks out of the room.

The door slams behind her.

I am alone.

Sticks and stones
APRIL 17

my grandma came to see me yesterday. i told my
mom about it and she started to cry. she thinks i'm
crazy, that i make things up to hurt her. i wish i had
someone in my life who believed me.

–E

16

KIKI

I hear Chrissy walk out of the room behind me in a huff. She looks at me for a second before shrugging, shaking her head and stalking to the stairwell. She pushes through the door and I turn to see Emma has almost reached the elevator. I run to catch up.

"Wait!" I call.

She slams her finger on the Down button.

"We're not supposed to go anywhere alone," I say, reaching out to grab her hand. She tightens her fingers into a fist.

"Don't . . . do that," she says.

"Do what?" But my fingertips tingle. I've never thought too much about how often I touch Emma, casually, like it's no big deal. She's never minded before.

"Come on." She glares. I swallow hard. "You napped with me in the bed."

"You told me to," I say defensively.

"You're always grabbing my hand, following me around, batting your eyes at—" She cuts herself off. "It's not like I'm blaming you or anything, but you just don't get it. It means more to me than it does to you."

"Why would it—"

"Ha!" She isn't amused. That's super clear from the way her nostrils flare like a pissed-off bull in a fight. "Get a clue, Kiki."

The elevator doors open and she steps on.

"I *do* have a clue. I'm not just some sparkly trophy, you know?"

"I never said you were. I just wish you'd stop playing dumb with me." The doors start to close, but Emma extends her hand to stop them. "Master key. I might need it to find the cameras."

I'm too shook to argue. I unzip my fanny pack and hand the key over, careful not to touch her when I do. I turn around, unable to look back at her as the elevator doors close. I feel her eyes on me as the doors separate us and the elevator takes her away.

Emma and I met in ninth-grade English class. She didn't much care for me at first. I always thought it was because I'm flaky and not all that serious about school. But when we started hanging out during Ghost Gang shoots, she warmed up. She seemed to admire me, to be impressed with how I was helping grow the channel, landing influencer deals and collabs.

She actually agreed with me about politics and religion and women's stuff. She valued my takes; she thought they were cool and smart.

She appreciated my people skills. She's the one who first acknowledged my magical powers of persuasion. One reason I can do what I do is because she believes in me.

She's become more important to me than I thought possible

for someone with an ever-present resting bitch face and zero interest in shopping.

But we're not more than friends.

I mean—how could we be? I've never even kissed a girl. Or anyone, for that matter.

Emma's lips flash through my mind.

I don't know how that makes me feel, and I really don't think now is the right time to figure it out.

No, you know what? Screw her for putting me on the spot like this. There is a serial killer on the loose, two people are dead, and my friends are in danger.

Including Emma.

I slam the Down button with my finger. If we've lost all our cameras and footage, maybe there's a way I can use my magic to get to access the hotel security feeds.

Maybe then Emma will see I'm not so clueless. Not useless. Still worth her time.

I huff, squaring my shoulders. I shouldn't even care what she thinks at all.

* * *

CHRISSY

The fluorescent light in the stairwell hurts my eyes. I tromp up two flights before pausing to breathe. My chest is tight, and every breath feels strained and restricted.

And that's before I see the man standing in the corner wearing pajama pants. His hair is slick like oil; his teeth are small and worn; his face is pockmarked.

He scratches at the scars on his face, his eyes vacant.

There's no one else around to ask whether he's real. Did he meet his death in this stairwell years ago? Or is he a current Hearst resident and I'm a stupid seventeen-year-old who stumbled on him accidentally?

I decide making eye contact is the wrong decision.

I turn around and go down a flight, exiting the stairwell on floor five instead of four. When I'm safely on the other side of the door, I lean back against the wall, breathing slowly to steady my racing nerves. My eyes flutter closed, and I'm immediately back in our room, replaying the argument.

Chase.

The look on his face when I called him out . . . I tried to play it off like his feelings didn't matter to me, but the truth is I'm not just pissed that he accused Bram of lying, I'm angry that he won't admit he's jealous.

The day I met Chase Montgomery I couldn't stop staring at his floppy hair and the V of his collarbones. He had on a vintage Hawaiian-print tank top and a pair of white-and-gray striped shorts. He kept running his hand through his hair and tucking it behind his ears. Finally, after his hair fell into his eyes too many times, he said, "Screw it," and used his shades as a headband.

Then I couldn't stop staring at his eyes.

Warm and kind, with dark lashes.

He ordered us pizza and paid, and I knew it wasn't a date because it was for a school project. I didn't even want it to be a date because I was new in town and Chase was the first person to talk to me. The first person to make eye contact, who didn't snicker behind my back. Turned out he was just as kind as his eyes.

I kick my combat boot against the wall, my lids popping open.

The fifth floor is one of the nicer ones in the hotel. The carpets are cleaner; they look like they've actually been vacuumed recently. The wallpaper isn't peeling. There are even working lightbulbs in all the hallway sconces.

This must be one of the floors where the less budget-conscious tourists stay.

Down the hallway I see the elevators. The lights aren't moving up on any of them. One moves down to the lobby at a slow clip.

When the elevator dings and the doors open, cold settles at the base of my spine. A chilly, unnatural warning.

The elevator is empty.

I push myself off the wall to face the open doors.

"Hello?" The word slips out like I'm a girl in a slasher film calling out to the killer. She always says her boyfriend's name next, tells him how this isn't funny, she's not kidding.

I don't do any of that.

I take one step and then another closer to the elevator, craning my neck to try to get a look inside it. I can see from the mirror on its back wall that there isn't anyone in the car. Unless they are small enough to hide in the corner by the elevator panel.

There was a TikTok that Kiki showed me over spring break, after we decided to make it our goal to reach Hearst by Halloween. She and I had been swimming most of the afternoon, and we'd gotten out of the pool so I could reapply sunscreen for the tenth time.

In the video, the girl was spooked. Not social media spooked, where girls are still cute and have all their mascara on.

She was legit terrified to her core.

She'd played this elevator game that's supposed to allow you to briefly pulse between this realm and the next. The game entails tapping in a specific floor combination on the number panel to either be given a chance to briefly sojourn in the "other world" or encounter a disturbing presence in the form of a woman on the fifth floor.

I flick my eyes to the room door nearest me.

553

My mouth goes dry.

Eileen Warren blogged about playing the elevator game with friends at the Plaza Hotel in New York City when she was in high school. Nothing happened, and she blew it off as a hoax, but in the footage that the LAPD released of her from the night she disappeared, she appeared to press the same numbers in the same order as needed to trigger the game play.

If Eileen was psychic, she wouldn't play with the spiritual realms like that, which makes me think there was something else going on.

The elevator doors hang open, as if someone is holding them just for me.

My breath swirls in gray smoke through the air.

My fingers ache with the cold.

The woman you meet in the game is never, ever, under any circumstances, to be spoken to.

I force my eyes to stay open. *Don't blink.*

Close, I beg the doors. *Please close.*

The mirror inside the elevator fogs up.

My eyes water, begging me to blink. Just once, and fast.

Close.

Open.

Her eyes are black holes in her head.

Empty caverns, an abyss.

She's in a wet old-fashioned dress with a muddy hem.

Her hair is long, knotted, drenched.

I exhale, and her lips twist in a smile. The doors close.

I drop against the wall, sliding down it, taking shallow swift breaths, in and out, in and out, until I can't see my breath anymore.

I can't help but wonder if that was the last face Eileen Warren saw before she died.

17

CHASE

Three a.m. is when the weirdos come out at the Hearst.

Which is good news for me. When Linda leaves her office to break up a fight in the lobby, I'm able to sneak inside undetected.

This is some high-level avoidance, but it's better than chasing after Chrissy when she explicitly told me not to or emptying the contents of Bram's backpack to see what other secrets he's hiding in there.

Chrissy would rather accuse me of orchestrating this entire trip to kill people for YouTube subs than admit there's a possibility—even a tiny sliver of a chance—she could be wrong about Bram.

I know she's into him, and I can hardly blame her.

Not because he's *sextacular* or *swoony* or whatever word people use nowadays to describe mysterious dudes with accents and six-packs.

But because he's like her.

I've always thought of Chrissy's psychic abilities as a blessing, but I know she thinks of them as a curse. It must be something to share a curse with someone. She must feel seen and understood by Bram. Or Roy, or whatever his real name is.

I can never compete with that.

I pull back Linda's chair to see that she's left her laptop open, but it's dropped into sleep mode. Of course. My luck is not of the Irish variety, despite my dad's family being from the Emerald Isle. My gran was racist as hell and never missed a chance to act insulted by my mom's Filipino ancestry. Lucky for her, she died before I started putting full sentences together; otherwise, I would've really given her something to feel insulted about.

I touch the space bar and the screen illuminates. It's password protected. I guess I should expect a criminal kingpin to be paranoid.

I wish the rest of the Ghost Gang were here to help.

But they're not. I'm on my own. I guess I'll have to use some old-fashioned detective skills—which I'm not sure I actually possess—to figure this out.

My eyes flick over the surface of the desk.

Sometimes, people write their passwords on Post-its and stick them to the underside of a coaster or a paperweight or something. Linda has both. The coaster is from the Hard Rock Cafe at the Mall of America, which is so random and weird I actually have a pang of sympathy for this possible sociopath.

The paperweight is a blue butterfly trapped in resin, and it feels symbolic somehow, that this horrible woman would keep one of nature's most beautiful creatures trapped in plastic on top of her messy desk.

Of course, both the coaster and the paperweight come up empty.

I pull open a desk drawer, carefully shifting through the slew of papers inside as I search. I find a picture of Linda and Steve from what looks like a few years ago. They're just as disheveled and odd-looking, but slightly less wrinkled. They definitely had a weird vibe between them, but could Linda really be responsible for her own son's murder?

I keep searching.

Behind me is a bookcase filled with file folders and other stuff that looks like normal, boring office crap. I root around the shelves for a few minutes until I find a copy of *The Shining* on top of a stack of romance paperbacks. It's the only horror novel on the shelf, and appears to be the only hardcover book Linda owns.

I flip through it and stuck right beneath the line "This inhuman place makes human monsters" like it's underlining it, is a creased and faded yellow Post-it. There's what looks like a PIN written on it, and underneath that is *redrum20031*. I wonder briefly whether the number holds some kind of significance, but I don't care enough to try to crack the code.

I put the book back where I found it and brush one finger over the laptop track pad until the box for the password appears. I type in the password and hold my breath. Honestly, I'm not sure what I'm hoping to find, but at least if I try to find *something* that points to what Linda's up to, then maybe my friends will forgive me for pointing out the fact—because it is a *fact*—that Bram's name on his passport doesn't match the name he gave us.

Linda's computer desktop is disorderly—no surprise there, considering the state of everything else in this hotel. Things are saved randomly and not organized into folders. Without digging too deep I can tell that finding anything useful could take hours.

Hours that I don't have.

I hear a voice coming from the hallway leading into the office. Linda's voice. Irritated.

Fuuuck.

This is a one way in, one way out office. I have to find somewhere to hide.

Fast.

...

KIKI

"Picture this, though," Joe the security guard is saying, eyes bright and starry.

I've managed to distract him from the fact that I am not returning his skeleton key by asking him about the plot of his screenplay.

"Buck Parson is just your average, slick, handsome-as-all-heck Black man living in the city. He moved here to become a world-renowned DJ"—Joe scratches out a beat on an imaginary record—"but took a job as a hotel security guard to pay the bills."

His screenplay is titled *Buck Parson vs. the Grim Reaper,* and if you removed the scythe-wielding harbinger of death, I'm pretty sure it's just Joe's life story plus rock-hard pecs and a phase gun that can capture the wandering souls of the undead.

"It's midnight," Joe continues, "the devil's hour, they call it, and as the clock chimes ominously, the Grim appears. Now the only one standing between the sleeping hotel guests and death is Buck Parsons, security guard with impeccable rhythm."

My plan was to get Joe talking about his masterpiece and, once he was rolling in the warm fuzzies, ask him to print me a copy, leaving me alone with the security camera feed.

That was ten minutes ago, and he hasn't so much as stopped to breathe between plot points. I am running out of time.

"But I thought you said the final battle is between Buck and the Lady in White?"

"She's the one pulling the strings," Joe says.

I don't think he understands much about hauntings, which is probably a good thing considering he works in a haunted hotel. If he were more alert to the goings-on of the super-natural, he might be too scared to show up for his shifts.

I grin and nod, maintaining my furrowed brow.

"It's hard to picture without the words in front of me," I say. This gets the look of pure joy I was hoping for.

"I got a copy on my computer," Joe says, pointing at a rough-looking messenger bag hung over the back of a chair against the wall. "There's a printer up front. Ms. Morton doesn't mind me using it when she's not."

Ms. Morton is Linda. I bet she makes all the hotel staff call her Ms. Morton. Screw her.

"I'd love to read it," I say, smiling. "My friends have all passed out, but I can't sleep." I feel a stab of hurt when I say *friends*. We've never split up like this before, not since we all agreed to follow the Ghost Code. "I need something to pass the time."

The elation that brightens Joe's eyes at my request is almost enough to make me wish I wasn't lying. The likelihood I can read his screenplay tonight (or ever) is minimal, and I really hate lying to such a nice man who seems genuinely passionate about his pursuit of a screenwriting career.

Maybe I'll read it. If we make it out of this place alive.

Joe smacks his knees with his palms and pops up.

"Be back in a jiff!" he says, grabbing a giant ancient laptop from his messenger bag and traipsing out the door.

As soon as his footfalls are far enough away, I drop down in his chair to get the lay of the land—camera-wise.

My eyes drift to the elevator cam that's positioned awkwardly to face the button panel in the car we've been using most of the night. The same car that security footage had captured Eileen Warren riding in the night she disappeared.

The same car that they found her remains in.

And now, the same car that Emma rides in, alone, and still without a camera in hand. My finger touches the screen, right where her fuzzy grainy face scowls at the mirror that covers the back wall.

Could I be into Emma as more than "just friends"? I think back to what she said earlier—that every time I grab her hand or hug her, it means more to her than it does to me. But how could she possibly know what it means to me when I'm not even sure?

I blink and refocus on the footage. Each TV has a primitive tape deck that probably has a videotape inside recording everything. I just need to locate the one that might give me a look at the locations of interest.

Locations that are not the elevator Emma is riding in at this moment.

...

EMMALINE

After raging over the debacle in our room and my stupid almost-reveal of my *stupid* unrequited attraction to Kiki, I searched the dumpster in the alley behind the hotel with my phone flash-light. My gut instinct is that the killer trashed the cameras along with the murder weapon, and since the alley behind the Hearst is practically deserted, and probably cursed, it seemed a likely location. Ritter used to strip off his bloody clothes outside and then toss them in the dumpster after a long night of stalking.

No one cared then. Not much has changed since.

The cameras weren't in the dumpster, at least not close to the top, and I wasn't about to dive in and ruin my kicks. If they are in there, then my next hypothesis is that whoever stole the cameras did so hastily, considering there couldn't have been much time between the murder and us finding Steve's body. They wouldn't have had time to stash the cameras far from the scene of the crime.

I'm riding the elevator back up to floor four, where I plan to focus my search for the time being. If we're going to pin this on Linda, the cameras could be anywhere because she has key access. It means endless possibilities, which I really hate.

At least I got the master key from Kiki.

The hurt-puppy-dog look on her face flashes through my mind.

I shouldn't have snapped at her, and not just because searching the hotel for two spy cameras would have been a lot easier with some help. I shouldn't have snapped because this is my problem, not Kiki's. I like her and I need to get over it. Either she likes me back or she doesn't.

Typically, I'm as neutral as Switzerland. Unromantic, unemotional.

Besides the one girlfriend I had for all of junior year, I've never really been the bare-your-soul-and-say-I-love-you type. Gilly, said girlfriend, had my heart for a lot longer than I expected for a high school relationship. One year and four months. And despite how much I cared about her, that relationship still ended in a spectacular emotional crash.

I mean, for her. Remember, Swiss, baby.

Kiki is cooler than me in almost every way. The opposite of a trophy.

She's smarter than most of the world gives her credit for and a better, more selfless human than the rest of our team, even quiet psychic empath Chrissy.

The elevator doors slide open for me to exit.

Two girls stumble from a room and leave the door hanging open. They're clearly drunk as they walk down the hallway toward me, and as soon as they pass, I hear one say in a heavy Russian accent, "Hey, baby."

I roll my eyes hard and don't look back.

I do have the decency to close their door, for their safety and the safety of their belongings. One of them calls out a slurred, "Thanks, girrrl!" as the elevator doors close on them. I continue in the direction of the bathroom.

I don't need Kiki to like me back. I don't.

I need hi-def footage of a murderer in the act of slaying.

...

The curtains are musty and caked with dust, but at least they hide me.

"Screw you and Turner," Linda says. While listening to her call I learn that she swears like a sailor and doesn't think too highly of cops, the mayor of LA or the "Hollywood elite," as she calls them.

She's been on the phone for about three minutes. I started recording as soon as she said, "I have the goods. I'll keep them here until sunrise."

What goods?

"I'm not changing the price. We need to renovate the pool, and how am I going to make that happen if I keep cutting you deals?"

As far as I can tell, she's talking to a client about her side hustle. I wish she'd come right out and say what she's peddling, because while there's no denying the entirely suspect nature of whatever it is, there's also nothing concrete to accuse her of. She hasn't said the numbers of the rooms where the merch is stashed. She hasn't said anything that I can follow up on later.

She also hasn't mentioned Anna or Steve.

"Wonder-freaking-ful," she says, and I hear the smile in her voice without having to see it cut across her face. "Steve isn't here tonight, so you'll be dealing with me directly."

Steve *was* here tonight.

Linda doesn't say a word about her son heading home early, or going missing from his regular front-desk duties, which makes me think she's not worried about his sudden disappearance.

And if she didn't kill him, shouldn't she be worried?

I hear the desk chair slide back and squeak loudly as Linda sits back in it. There's a metallic flick, and then I smell skunk burning.

Great, I'm stuck in here with a probably-murderer-definite-criminal, and now I'm gonna smell of dust, mold *and* weed. Plus, I can't even text anyone to get a diversion going so I can bail out before the stench settles in my hair because all my friends think I'm a giant jealous jerk.

Maybe it's time to admit to myself that I'm the one to blame for this shit show.

Not Bram.

18

CHRISSY

The room's a bit lacking in human beings

This is the text from Bram when I finally peel my eyes open. My breathing has normalized and the temperature in the hall is back to balmy, but my heart still flutters a little too fast for my liking. I don't want to look, but I have to be sure the elevator doors stayed closed and that *thing* inside stayed gone.

I let out a weak sigh of relief.

She wasn't a ghost. She was worse. She was wholly unnatural.

I push myself up from the floor with my fingertips and then lean back against the wall.

We're fighting, is all I text to Bram.

He's typing a response; I can tell by the three blinking dots. I really don't want to explain why we're fighting because it will mean the awkward reveal of Chase going through Bram's back-pack and not so subtly accusing him of lying and, by extension, murder.

He sends a 😕 followed by a request for my location.

Something moves in my peripheral vision, tugging my focus from my phone to the stairwell door.

Not something.

Someone.

A girl, probably my age or a little younger.

She's wearing a dirty T-shirt with the word *Summer* written on it in script. Right where a rainbow appliqué curves beneath the letters is a huge tear. She has an untied white tennis shoe on one foot; her other foot is bare. Her wrists have welts from what I'm guessing were some kind of restraints.

I feel a stab of certainty like a knife in my heart. She was tied up. She was held. She was strangled.

The bruises on her neck show faintly in her shifting form.

She's here and then not, a soft shape of bruised flesh and broken hope. There and then gone, like her signal is weak.

The temperature drops again, and my stomach swims. I remove the beanies, first Emma's and then mine, and as I do, the girl's form solidifies, even though I know it's not solid. (Not on this plane of existence at least.)

Strangled, discarded. Just like Anna. Just like the girl I saw in the pizza parlor. Just like the one who was with me on the elevator when I saw Eileen's body.

Trash. The words belt me in the stomach and I almost double over.

The girl twists her hands in her shirt, trying to cover her exposed stomach.

Ritter strangled his victims, all of them young women. Linda and the Hearst have some kind of twisted connection. Maybe the spirits stuck here are trying to help me help them.

The ghost lifts one finger, curling it, beckoning me.

My head feels hollow but clear. *Follow me.* I don't hear the words so much as feel them all the way through me, like a chill running down the length of my spine.

She nods her head toward the door behind her, and then she's gone to the other side. Her pale face, marked with purple bruises, stares at me from the window in the door.

I shove my phone in my pocket and follow her.

...

KIKI

No surprise, but Hearst's security footage has hella annoying blind spots.

None of them are in great locations, and none are in the location I need: ice and vending, or the general area around ice and vending, or floor fourteen. In fact, the best footage I've been able to get is of the lobby and—surprise, surprise—the area just outside Linda's office.

She walked into her office on the phone a little while ago and hasn't emerged since.

I flick my eyes over the screens. One of the cameras is on a rotation, switching from the back alley entrance, where there's a dumpster, to the roof, then to a fire escape—my guess is it's floor fourteen since it's closest to the roof and the most common location that residents and visitors use to access the roof.

I'm watching the screen flip from the alley to the fire escape when I get a text in the group chat.

apologies pending but can someone come help me escape Linda's office

she's smoking up

Chase is trapped in Linda's office. Alone. Committing sins against the Ghost Code, just like the rest of us.

I don't text back that *this is exactly why we have the buddy system,* because I don't want Linda to hear Chase's phone buzz. I hope Chase turns off his phone in case someone else doesn't have the brainpower to realize the same thing.

I shoot up, spin on my heels and run from the room. Straight into Joe.

The pages of his screenplay cascade to the ground.

"Oof," he says, and then our eyes meet. "You're in an awful hurry and I thought—"

I grab him by the shoulders and look him square in the eyes.

"Get that script back in order for me, Joe," I say, as serious as death. "If I make it to morning, I'll come back for it."

I release him and run down the hall as he calls after me.

"Why wouldn't you make it until morning?"

...

EMMALINE

The smell is what drags my attention away from the search.

Brownies and beer. The *thomp* of electronica. The laughter of a crew that is definitely high on something besides life.

The fire escape was a dead end. So was the bathroom. The first three rooms I tried were empty.

I need a burger, but I'll settle for whatever I can get.

The room where the party is in full swing is two doors down from ours. It's a lot to ask me to resist right now when everything is so fucked up and I'm hangry as hell.

Outside the party-room door a guy is sitting on the ground, a girl on top of him. He's got a set of silver rings on his left hand, which clutches her hip. The right slides up into her dark hair.

"Like what you see?" he asks me between nipping kisses over her neck.

Not even a little, but that doesn't stop me from looking.

The room is twice the size of ours, with six bunks and two large closets. I can tell the closets are bigger than the ones in our room because the double doors of one closet are open. Inside, a guy wearing a big hat with dramatic fringe has set up a tarot table. A disco ball lit up with neon lights that send streams of color through the room hangs over his head.

It's so dark that I can't make out how many people are in the room, but I do see brownies and drinks set up on top of one of the bunk beds. I walk over to a girl who's pouring herself another round in a red Solo cup. She's pretty, with long dark hair and a septum piercing. The ring is black and metallic. She lifts the bottle of rum, shrugging one shoulder.

"Want?" she asks me. She's wearing a costume, something from the Spider-verse sans the mask—I'm not exactly familiar with comic book heroes. She fills out the suit well, but right now I'm eyeing the brownies behind her.

"Those are laced," she says. "Beware." She waggles her eyebrows. "Unless you're into that."

"Rum it is," I say, grabbing a Solo cup. She pours the alcohol in straight and cracks open a can of Coke. The liquid fizzes up and then slowly crackles down. The girl raises her cup toward me and we cheers. I watch as she takes a long drink before doing the same, just to make extra certain the contents are clean.

Her shiny eyes drag over my face.

"You staying on this floor?" she asks. I nod. "You know this is *her* floor."

"Her?" I ask, sipping gingerly from my cup.

"The crazy chick," she says, one eyebrow hooked up. She means Eileen, and I'm pretty sure if Kiki were here, she'd correct the girl's use of both *crazy* and *chick*. "My friend Connor is trying to contact the spirit world."

"Connor?" I follow her eyes to the guy sitting under the disco ball with a tarot deck stacked in front of him on a card table. "I thought that was a joke."

Her eyes go wide in mock surprise. "We never joke about the dead, especially here." She giggles. I roll my eyes and she doubles down. "He's really good at just, like, reading normal card spreads, though."

"A guy named Connor is good at tarot?" I don't buy it. She grabs me by the arm and tugs me across the room. She presents me to Connor with another giggle.

"She's a skeptic," the girl says. Connor looks up through the haze. His pupils are dilated, most likely because he's on something. I'm not sure he actually sees me. He motions for me to sit. The girl pushes me into the chair.

The last thing I need today is another psychic. Real or fake.

"I'm not interested," I groan. As a practice, there's nothing wrong with tarot conceptually, but I've personally never seen the need for a card to tell me what my gut usually can.

Connor looks up at the girl. "Let me work, Gina."

"Don't be a dick, Connor," she scoffs. He glares. "Whatever." She walks off and disappears into the darkness. Connor leans in.

"Humor me, I'm trying to learn."

I shrug, which earns a grin from the wannabe medium-in-training. I take another swig of my rum and Coke.

"Cut the deck three times."

* * *

KIKI

This is what you were born for, Kiki.

Not this exactly. I was born for fame and international acclaim, but my charm, that je ne sais quoi that draws people's eyes and keeps them watching, is a major through line in the biography of Kiki Lawrence.

I'm a mirrorball . . . shining just for you . . . Taylor Swift gets me.

I can get anyone to like me, even maybe-murderous mother-managers.

I stand at the deserted front desk. The clock that hangs above it *tick ticks* quietly and the sound is ominous and hollow. There's evidence of an incident, because a housekeeper with tired eyes and wearing hospital workers' shoes mops up the floor where it looks like someone threw up. Or worse.

I tap my palm on the metal bell, hoping Linda will hear it from her office, which I can only assume is somewhere through the arched doorway behind the desk.

Ding. I wait a second, listening for movement. When there isn't anything audible, I peer around the corner. There's a door ajar, and it is definitely the right hallway—I recognize it from the video footage. *Dingdingdingdingding*—

"Jesus Christ on a cross," a voice exclaims. I feel like I should cross myself just to be safe and I'm not even religious. The smell of a burning joint reaches me before Linda does. She's left the joint behind, but its stench follows her, probably from the smoke captured by her bottle-blond rat's nest of hair set with hair spray.

Her face falls when she sees me.

"You're one of the nosy little shits from room 421, aren't you?" She inspects me unapologetically.

"I don't know what you mean by that," I say, batting my lashes.

"You guys said there was funny business on floor fourteen."

Guys. I mentally give her the middle finger.

"You must have confused me with someone else," I say. Smile. "I just got back from West Hollywood and now I need a shower."

She crosses her arms. She knows I'm lying.

"There aren't any towels in my room and I need one," I press on.

Chase appears behind her in stealth mode, shoes in hand to keep from making any noise on the tile floor. His eyes look a little bleary, like they're readjusting to the light. They land on me with a wild expression that's a mixture of gratitude and terror.

"I'm beat and I just need a shower and a good night's sleep," I say. Linda looks at her watch. "I sleep late."

"Checkout is at eleven a.m. *sharp*," she says, frowning.

"I set an alarm." I show my teeth with a smile.

"Need any soap or shampoo?"

Chase makes his escape, ducking around the far edge of the counter and dropping out of sight behind it. I force a poker face, but inside I'm happy and dancing to Lizzo's "Good as Hell," because that's how I'm feelin' at the success of my stealth rescue mission.

Linda tosses me a towel that is rougher than sandpaper.

Even though I'm not sure someone like her could kill her own son in cold blood, I also wouldn't put it past her.

JUNE 30

i'd do anything for a friend to take the pressure off

–E

19

EMMALINE

Medium-in-training Connor has a shtick, he explains, and since I still have some rum and Coke left, I let him give it to me. He says I need to focus my energy in order to get the cards to give me "insight and clarity" and "not just be bullshit." Without meaning to, I find my mind tripping back over the events of the night so far.

I always thought I was too smart to end up in a slasher movie. The girls in them are usually dumb, save the virginal one, who is allowed to live.

Connor flips the first of the three cards. His face screws up the moment his eyes land on it. I look at it too, but since this is my first-ever tarot reading, I'm not sure what I'm seeing. A blond dude tripping along in life.

I scowl. Connor mirrors my expression.

"What's the deal?" I ask, chugging the rest of my drink. "I'm gonna guess by your face, this isn't as silly as it seems."

"It's not silly. The cards aren't silly," he says, snippy. But then his lips twitch, nerves making them tighten. "It depends on what else you drew from the deck."

"The Fool," I read out loud. I blink, annoyed. "I'm at the top of my class."

"It's not about intelligence," Connor snaps, eyeing me closely. "It's about your attitude. You don't take things seriously."

"Wrong," I say, unimpressed. "I'm dead serious." But it's a lie, and Connor can tell.

"You deflect a lot," he says.

It's stupid to think about Kiki right now, but I do. I lift my cup to my lips, only to find it's empty. I drop my gaze to the second card.

"Next," I grunt.

"Fine." Connor turns it over and looks curiously like he's starting to regret practicing on me.

Until the color drains from his face. His eyes land on mine.

The card shows a man facedown with ten swords plunged into his back. His red cape is pulled back, and the sky above him is black and foreboding.

I have to hard-gulp the saliva that's just filled my mouth.

"Okay, that doesn't look good," I croak, feigning disinterest. Connor doesn't look like he buys my disinterest, however.

"Uh, not great, no," he says, wetting his lips. He leans in. "There's some different vibes you can go with on this one, but, like, none of them are good. It usually means something bad is happening or is going to happen. But not just bad, like a full-on ultimate low point."

"Like death?" I ask.

"I don't feel comfortable saying yes to that." He pauses. "Or no. Let's just say if you haven't recently experienced a sudden blow, get ready for one."

Great.

"If I saw someone who had died, could that be why this card turned up?" I ask, a glimmer of hope leaking into my voice. Connor shrugs one shoulder. Great. "Super not reassuring, thanks, dude."

We both flick our eyes to the third and final card.

"I don't have to keep going," he says. The quiver in his voice suggests that he doesn't want to see how this ends.

"We're in too deep," I say. "Might as well go all the way."

He presses his fingertips to the card, huffs out air between his lips and flips it.

The Hanged Man. That's a disturbing name, but as far as the spread is concerned at least it looks like he's having an okay time—or as much of an okay time as a person can have while dangling upside down. His eyes are wide open and staring, and he's suspended by one ankle, his arms tied behind his back.

Okay, so overall, not super great.

I look at Connor. He is biting into a brownie he must have stashed back there. Guess this is getting too intense for him.

"This"—he chews, staring at me—"could be worse."

"Awesome?" I don't feel reassured in the slightest. Two stars on Yelp for Medium Connor.

"So, it's about putting yourself in an uncomfortable position where fighting won't help you." He touches the spot where the man's arms are tied behind him. "You just gotta let go, 'cause you can't win."

If Connor knew that right now I'm hunting for cameras

with possible footage of a murder, he might not be so flippant about this letting-go thing.

I let go and who knows what could happen.

"This is all about release," he carries on, chomping another bite.

My stupid brain shoots to the fight the Ghost Gang had, and me walking out on my friends.

"Basically, you gotta take one for the team." My eyes fly to Connor's face, which looks hopeful. "It could be the exact solution to whatever ominous shit is happening with the other cards."

My skin prickles with goose bumps.

Or it could be the end of everything I care about the most.

20

CHRISSY

The ghost stays ahead of me the whole time we climb the stairs.

Up one flight, then another.

The higher we go, the more my head spins.

"Where are you taking me?" I ask her finally, as I slide my arms into the sleeves of my cardigan. The cold hasn't let up since we entered the stairwell.

She stops, twitching one hand. She can't answer—I know she can't answer, but when she moves her hand, I smell something. Sharp, pungent, salty.

She's bone-dry, but I smell the ocean.

I close my eyes, rubbing the exhaustion out of them until they start to water. I roll them open and stare directly into a different pair of eyes. Broken blood vessels splinter the whites like spiderwebs. The brown pupils are muted and glassy.

Moisture beads on this girl's skin. Her long hair is wet. Her tan is light, the kind you have at the beginning of summer, before you've spent any time in the sun.

She's wearing the same swimsuit she wore in the elevator,

right after I saw Eileen Warren's blood dripping from the ceiling grate.

The girl walks backward up the stairs. The effect is like when you rewind an old videotape, the kind my grandma had in the kids' playroom back home. Her limbs make jerking motions; her hair swishes, but it's stiff, not fluid. Not alive.

When I look back at the ghost I followed into the stairwell, her hands are balled into fists.

More.

I feel the word, and I know it's her trying to tell me something.

The girl in the polka-dot bathing suit leans over the railing, watching us. The ghost and I look up at her. And that's when I know these two souls are connected.

Killed by the same person or because of the same person.

Linda may not be doing the actual strangling, but maybe she's leading these girls to their death. Maybe Anna was caught in the cross fire.

"I know another girl died tonight," I say. "I need to find her body."

The girl in the *Summer* shirt turns to face me and tugs on the hem of her shirt, trying to hide the skin exposed where the shirt has ripped.

The smell of the ocean is gone as quickly as it came.

The girl looks at me, not through me. The dead would rather not see the differences between them and the living, but she's not turning away.

"I want to help," I say.

Sometimes they want to hurt you. Sometimes they want you to help them stop hurting.

She turns around and starts walking again. I tighten my cardigan around me to keep out the cold, but I know the decreasing temperature means she's not leaving just yet. Her presence is strong, and the stronger she feels, the better my chances of locating Anna's body.

My phone buzzes in my pocket, and I realize I've missed calls and texts. There are a few from Bram, asking where I am so he can meet up with me because he's got some intel that I might want to hear. And there's one from Chase in the group chat, asking to be rescued and promising to apologize (but not actually doing it).

I fire off a text to Bram:

I'm following a lead of my own
not sure where
U can come try to keep up

I don't wait for him to confirm or ask for more details. I shove my phone in my pocket and follow the ghost up the stairs.

...

CHASE

There's blood on my shoelaces.

I didn't notice it before, and for some reason it's the thing that finally makes me crack.

My mom got me these sneakers the week before school started. She took me to Miracle Mile Shops and we had lunch at Gordon Ramsay's Hell's Kitchen at Caesars Palace. It was the first time we'd talked in months for more than just a few sporadic sentences. We didn't even fight about Dad.

I press my palms to my eyes, trying to hold in the tears. Ever since I was a kid, I've loved horror. I dig true-crime docs and horror movies and haunted attractions. I wrote an essay titled "The Cultural Relevance of *The Blair Witch Project*" for film class.

Still, I've never wanted to see a dead body up close, not even in theory.

Tonight, I've seen two, and moved one from where it was dumped to a communal bathroom shower stall. Steve's blood is on the shoes that my mom bought me for my senior year of high school. I'm not sure how I go home and explain to her that there's a murdered man's blood on my favorite sneakers.

"Linda went back to her den." Kiki's voice breaks into my thoughts. "Probably to finish her joint." I turn my eyes up to her. Her face immediately drops.

"I'm really sorry for all this," I say, looking down at my bloodstained laces again.

She drops down beside me on the lobby couch.

"For being a jealous jerk?" she asks, setting the towel and shampoo samples in her lap. "Or for planning a trip the same weekend as a couple of murders?"

I crack a smile. "Both." I pause to fiddle with my shoelaces. "And for breaking the Ghost Code."

"We all broke it." Kiki shrugs. "You can get that blood out with a soak in cold water."

"Will that work for the image seared in my brain?" I quip half-heartedly. Her lips droop. "Thanks for coming to my rescue," I say.

She small-smiles and leans over to bump her shoulder

against mine. I snort a laugh that feels like a bubble of anxiety popping in my chest.

"Emma and I had a fight," Kiki says. She starts picking at a loose thread on the towel. "Do you think you can have romantic feelings for someone and not realize it?"

I feel my eyes go involuntarily wide. "Like *you* have romantic feelings for someone?"

Emma?

"I don't know," she says, letting out a huge sigh and falling back against the couch. "I just thought I liked to be close to her because she got me. She's smart and listens when I rant. . . ." She looks at me with big eyes. "Can you accidentally fall in love?"

I drop back against the couch too. "I hope so. Then maybe I'd have a chance in hell with Chrissy."

Kiki elbows me in the ribs. "You do have a chance with her. What? You think hot Aussie psychic detective Bram Kelly is permanent?"

What a résumé. "I think you mean Roy Walker," I point out.

"Not gonna help," she says, lips pursed. "The point is: he's temporary, and if you can't see that you aren't and that matters, especially where Chrissy's concerned, then I can't help you."

"Chrissy loves the Ghost Gang," I say, still feeling sorry for myself. Kiki whacks me across the crown of my head. "Ouch! That hurt—you have a ring on."

"Good, maybe it'll snap you out of your stupor, dumbass." I rub the back of my head. "You're not wrong that she loves the group, but, Chase, you *made* the gang. You believed her when no one else did and you helped us believe her too. And you're also kind of a stud."

"I am *not* a stud," I say, feeling my cheeks go warm.

"I'm not taking the bait. Stop fishing for compliments." But Kiki grins as she says this.

"Thanks," I say. "Maybe you're right." She preens. "I am a stud."

That gets me another elbow in the ribs.

"Did you find anything useful in Linda's office?" she asks.

"Maybe something? I recorded her while she was on the phone." I pull out my phone, swiping through it to show Kiki the recording. "We should find Emma and Chrissy."

"Get the gang back together," Kiki says. She pulls out her own phone and slides into the group chat.

We're stronger together. Even if the saying is clichéd, it holds.

●●●

EMMALINE

Screw Medium-in-Training Connor and his tarot deck.

I left the party room without giving him a glowing recommendation or quelling my anxiety with another rum and Coke. The fastest way out of this mess is finding the cameras, and I'll keep looking until sunrise and beyond if I have to.

"Take one for the team," I snort, traipsing down the hall to the next set of doors. I fiddle with the handle on one to check whether it's locked. Across the hall is another open-door party that looks and sounds like spillover from the other one.

When Chase asked me to join Ghost Gang, I was skeptical and not just because of the whole psychic thing. Up to that point I had been all about the lone-wolf life and really saw no reason to change it. Then I got sucked into the channel, and the lives of these three other people started to matter more than my solitude.

I use the master key to unlock the room door. It's dark inside, and I can tell from the smell that no one has been in here in a while. But I do a quick sweep under the bunks and in the closet just to be safe.

When I go back into the hallway, a drunk girl stumbles out of a different room and right into me. Her breath smells tart like lemonade but with an edge.

"Hey there," she breathes into my face.

"You should drink some water," I say. She rolls her eyes, preparing a slurred argument, but her gag reflex kicks in and she shoots off in the direction of the bathroom.

I never thought I needed anyone, and I low-key resent how much I've come to rely on the Ghost Gang.

Not that I want them to know that.

I check inside the girl's room. There's a couple halfway undressed and making out with no awareness another person has entered the room. I'm able to easily search the room for our missing gear without them taking any notice of me. It goes mostly okay until the girl drops her bra on my head as I'm using my phone's flashlight to check underneath the bed.

A text comes in from Kiki just as I step back into the dingy dank hallway.

We need to regroup

Then another.

Plz text back Ive saved Chase and we have info

I touch the reply box, but then, in my peripheral vision, I notice the dark sliver of an open door.

Not just any door. A supply closet door.

A supply closet door is not typically something left unlocked and ajar in a place like this, where it's most definitely at risk of being looted by both patrons and unsanctioned visitors.

I walk across the hall to the closet. My fingers touch the door, pushing it further open. I use the flashlight on my phone to take a good look inside. There are three large utility shelves stacked high with single-ply toilet paper, trash bags and other random hotel-room shit that you'd expect to find in a supply closet. In one corner a mop in a bucket is propped against the wall.

Right in the center of the shelf on the back wall is a clear trash bag smeared with what looks like blood.

My stomach lurches, and I shoot to the shelf to take a closer look. Yep, it is most definitely blood. I am almost a total idiot, because my fingers reflexively reach to grab the bag. I use my phone flashlight to get a better look and something catches my eye immediately.

The cameras are inside.

No doubt there are fingerprints on the bag.

This might be the only evidence we need to call the cops for our own get-out-of-jail-free card.

"Who needs to take one for the team now, Connor?"

The closet door closes behind me, leaving me in darkness except for the light of my phone.

A hard punch to my back knocks the wind right out of me. My phone drops to the floor with a loud *crack*.

It wasn't a punch. The warm wet liquid spreading across my back gives way to throbbing white-hot pain that shoots through my torso.

My body lurches. My hands tremble.

I feel like I'm about to be sick all over the floor, and I drop to my knees, grappling for my phone and my friends. My lifeline, life saviors.

The phone is kicked from my grip, and a heavy-soled shoe stomps down on my hand.

SEPTEMBER 29

i am always alone and somehow never alone.

—E

21

CHRISSY

The ghosts have drawn me all the way to the top of the stairwell, where the only unlocked door is the one that leads to floor fourteen. In front of the door is the girl in the *Summer* shirt, but now her back is to me. Through the small window in the door, I see the face of the swimsuit girl, her muddy brown eyes bloodshot, the bruise on her neck a cool gray-black.

My head pounds, and the throbbing matches my rapid unsteady heartbeat. To help me see the ghosts clearly, I haven't worn the beanies this whole climb. It was the right move. The move I needed to make for this to work. But I'm paying for it now.

I wipe my fingers under my nose and they come away red. I feel my blood touch my upper lip and taste the familiar metallic tinge on my tongue.

Summer shirt ghost girl is gone now, and I know she wants me to open the door.

The last time I was on this floor the spirits went out of control. I shove my beanie on my head for some measure of protection and grab the door handle, yanking it open. When I enter the hallway, I see the *Summer* shirt ghost again standing by the window at the far end of the hall. She points at the ceiling.

I crane my neck and look. Tucked into the dilapidated crown molding is a security camera positioned so that it's recording the window onto the fire escape.

The security guy that Kiki got the key off earlier wasn't paying close attention to the cameras, so I hope I'll be able to climb out the window without him noticing. I turn to face the ghost, and the lights dim and flicker in a few bursts before snuffing out completely.

The whole hallway gets eerily cold.

The elevator dings.

The electricity has gone out again, I can tell by the absence of whirring air conditioners and lights. The elevator doors slide open behind me. I have to dare myself to look even though I know that whatever I see can't possibly be real.

Inside the elevator, dressed in a pair of low-slung skinny jeans and a Ramones T-shirt, her long dark hair smooth and shiny, stands Eileen Warren. Her face is clean of blood and brain matter; her eyes are securely in their sockets. Her lips aren't twisted in horror; her limbs aren't crushed into a soup of muscle and bone. This isn't her as she died. This is her as she lived.

I don't know why she's here like this, but I'm so glad that she is.

Her eyes fix on me, and somehow I know little things about her. She was scared when she died. She was alone and she doesn't remember the moment it happened or why, she only remembers the feeling of climbing and thinking the way out was up.

Tears pool in my eyes, trapped by my lashes.

The door to room 1413 bangs open and closed.

Open and closed.

Open. *Slam.*

A scream cuts through the darkness. Then another, and another, echoing around me. They shake my soul. But the screams are in my head, not out here. It's only me who can hear them. I can't get away from the sound.

I join in, dropping to the ground and pressing my hands to my ears.

I scream and my blood goes cold in my veins. I scream and I feel the prickle of cold fingers touching my skin.

I scream and it rattles my soul loose in my body.

This is what Hearst wants from me. Fear that feeds the shadows, that makes them stronger and me weaker. I wrench my eyes open. The hallway lights flicker on and off. On and off.

On, dead girls reach out, mouths open. Teeth rot, skin hangs.

Off, darkness consumes.

On, I look at them and scream, but not from fear. From solidarity. I see each face, see the wounds left on their bodies from the rope or the wire, the twine or the phone cord coiled around and around to squeeze their life away.

I close my eyes again. Tears rush down my cheeks.

All screaming but my own stops.

"Hey, you, girl!" A man's voice cuts in. I peel my eyes open and realize the lights are back, the hum of the air conditioner has kicked back on. The man stares at me from his open door wearing ratty old sweatpants and nothing else. "You havin' a bad trip or what?"

I shake my head, swallowing hard. My throat is raw.

"You get right there, see?" he says. "You're too young to die."

Not in a place like the Hearst.

The thought sends a final harsh chill through my body.

He shuts the door with a grunt of disapproval, or concern— I can't tell which.

My phone buzzes again, but I ignore it. This feels personal. Between me and the spirits trapped in Hearst's horrible grip.

I have to jimmy the lock using my beanie for traction. The lock is rusty and doesn't want to turn. On the other side of the window, I see the ghost girls waiting for me to join them.

I wrench the lock open and try to shove the window up. Its rusty hinges screech and the window doesn't open all the way, but I manage to slide out through the space. The window drops back down with a smack.

I'm glad that I'm not afraid of heights, because when I peer over the edge of the railing it's thirteen stories straight down to an alleyway littered with garbage. On the street in front of the hotel, I see the edge of a neon pawnshop's Open sign. I hear traffic and honking horns.

It has to be past four a.m. by now, but human life downtown, however unsavory, is alive, pulsating at all hours.

The only thing that stands between me and the roof is a thin metal ladder.

The ghost girls are gone, but I know they want me to finish the climb. I close my palms over the railing and hook my foot in the first rung.

When I reach the top, a gust of wind whips over me. It's cooler up here, and I'm momentarily distracted by the twinkle of city lights spread out around me like a Lite-Brite. From here, downtown LA looks magical. Not like the kind of place you go to die, or someone sends you to be forgotten. It looks ripe and bright with possibility.

Beautiful, in its own complicated way.

It's only when I drag my attention from the skyline that I realize I'm alone on the roof. The ghost girls who led me up here are nowhere to be seen. Even when I tug the beanie from my head, they don't appear.

But they must have wanted me to come up here for a reason.

I survey the roof for spots where a body could easily be hidden. If Steve brought Anna up here, he would have needed help, but I can't assume he didn't have that. Without knowing the full story about the dealings of Hearst's management, I can't be sure that Linda doesn't have more people on the payroll helping her clean up her messes.

I check in the dark corners between the water towers positioned next to each other that take up a whole section of the roof. I search behind the banks of air conditioners that cool the building, and walk the length of the ledges, scanning as I move, wishing that the ghosts I usually try to ignore would be pushier for once.

"What the hell?" I ask once I've made a full circle around the roof. "Why bring me all the way up here for nothing?"

I spin around like a girl calling out to her killer in a '90s slasher flick.

My phone buzzes over and over and over.

Bram's name flashes on the screen.

"It was a dead end," I say when I answer. He sighs.

"I'm in that bloody stairwell," he says, "trying to find you." There's a pause and I feel him smiling into the phone. My smile is a reflex. "You aren't an easy one to catch."

"I'm on the roof," I say.

"Be there in a jiff." He hangs up.

I drop onto the concrete and cross my legs to wait.

This isn't how I wanted my search to end. I thought if the ghosts were leading me, they must want me to find Anna's body, but instead I'm alone on the roof without another lead or even a ghost girl in sight. It's enough to make me want to give up, or just call the cops and have them deal with all of this.

I flick open the group chat to see texts from Chase and Kiki. Emma hasn't responded yet either, but she goes dark when she gets pissed. We have that in common.

I touch the icon of Chase's face in the chat. It's a photo I took over the summer. He's wearing sunglasses and has a stupid white baseball cap on sideways. He's freshly tanned, and has a Popsicle in his mouth. We were on hiatus from the channel and spent the whole week in Chase's pool.

He didn't say why he set the photo as his profile pic, but psychic or not, I could have guessed. It's not because he looks good in the shot. It's because I took it.

The crunch of shoes on gravel draws my attention up from the phone.

Bram stands at the edge of the rooftop, wearing a look of both curiosity and sympathy. His lips tug up into a half smile when our eyes meet.

"What a view," he says, looking away to scan the downtown LA skyline.

"Not too bad from where I'm sitting, either," I say, feeling brazen. This gets his attention back on me. He eats up the ground between us, and when he reaches me, he sits, folding his long legs into a pretzel. He's close enough that I could just lean over if I wanted and follow through on that kiss we almost had before.

The pleasant fuzzy sound is back, and it's such a relief that I tug my beanie off and take a deep breath.

He's a liar. I hear Chase in my head and I really don't want to.

"You said you were following a lead," he says.

"Oh, yeah, I thought maybe they stashed Anna's body up here," I say. "But it was a dead end."

"It would be awfully hard to cart anyone up that ladder, I expect," Bram says, looking at the railing that hooks around the roof's edge. "Steve didn't seem like the strongest bloke."

"That's assuming it was Steve. He and Linda might have someone helping them do their dirty work." I pause, twisting the beanie in my hands. "Whatever that work is." A sharp sudden pain cuts through my temple.

"Shit!" I say, and press my palm to the spot.

Blood drips from my nose. It's warm and wet on my upper lip.

Bram's hands clutch my shoulders, and I hear his voice saying my name through the searing pain. I blink, trying to clear my vision, but for a second all I see is bright white light.

"Chrissy, come back to me," he says, his voice pleading. "Come back."

His fingers are calloused and warm when they wipe the blood from my lips. Then he tugs me into his arms, and the buzzing overtakes my senses, drowning out the pain until it's all I can hear.

In his arms I am safe. Not just because he's strong but because he's like me. We're not different. I breathe in the sweet smell of the detergent on his shirt, and it reminds me of summer sunlight and the ocean.

"I'm okay," I say, the words feeling like a foreign language on my lips. Bram leans back to get a better look at me.

"Blimey," he says, and I can't help but crack a smile.

"I have to ask you something," I say. His face goes quizzical. "Please don't hate me."

"Hate and love are just next-door neighbors, right?" His eyes are bright with humor. I try not to dwell on him using the word *love*.

"Chase went through your backpack," I say, making a cringe face.

"Ah," he says, clenching his jaw.

"He's all freaked out because you have a different name on your passport."

"Understandable," Bram says. "But it's a simple misunderstanding. I have a few different fake passports from my employers for jobs like this. Safety reasons."

I laugh. "That's what I said." I shake my head. "He's just grasping at straws."

"He's watching your back," Bram says. "A little too closely for my liking, but—"

"What—why?" I snort.

"I don't like competition," he says.

A bolt of heat shoots through me when his eyes drop to my lips. The feeling almost makes me forget we're supposed to be hunting a killer and we're running out of time.

22

KIKI

I hug the towels close, even though the scratchy terry-cloth isn't as soothing as a security blanket. It's the fourth time we've tried to call Emma, and she still hasn't picked up. It's totally her MO when she's pissed to put her headphones on and turn up some death metal while she times herself taking apart and putting back together junk electronics. It's how she copes with big feelings rather than facing them head-on.

Chase has been known to edge his way back into her good graces with a Snickers and a can of Fanta as a peace offering, but that can only happen when we know where she is. And right now, we don't.

"Chrissy isn't responding either," Chase says, and I can tell he's trying to maintain his chill for both our sakes. He flips one of the shampoo samples from Linda absently in his hand. "But I'm the one she's wishing was dead, so I guess I shouldn't be surprised she's not taking my calls."

"Don't say that," I scold him. "Not after the night we've had."

He's nonplussed by my discomfort.

"It's not like Emma to be radio silent this long," he says, flipping from his texts to his home screen and the Find My app. He shoots me a look. "Okay, don't be pissed."

He taps the icon, which reveals that he's set up our phones to share our locations with him without asking permission. His expression is sheepish. My face warms with anger.

"Before you judge me," he says when my mouth drops open in surprise, "I figured this would be useful if we ever got separated on location."

"How did you get into our phones?" My voice hikes up an octave.

"Kiki, your passcode is your dog's birthday."

"Sherlock is my best friend." I pout.

"Which makes his big day an obvious choice for a password," Chase counters. "Emma's is the first four numbers of pi in reverse, and Chrissy's is the date of her mom's death scrambled."

The fact that Chase easily ascertained this information and then surreptitiously used it *should* upset me, but it actually makes me feel all warm and fuzzy inside.

It's nice to have someone who knows you that well and still wants to see your face every day. But I still act grouchy about it.

"Fine," I say, giving in. Of course we're all showing up in the Hearst, but Chase isolates Emma's phone, hiding the rest.

"We'll track her icon until we're right on top of it," he says. "Let's take the stairs." He bolts up, cracking his neck like he's preparing to tap into a fight. I leave the towel on the couch but put the sample shampoos in my fanny pack.

"Might as well get your money's worth," I say, grinning.

"I'll be demanding a full refund on account of the double

murder," Chase says. I laugh and tuck my arm into the crook of his elbow.

We launch out in search of our friend.

■ ■ ■

Emma is somewhere on floor four, but when we reach the door to the fourth floor, we hear the pulsing sound of house electronica and heavy bass. Parties have broken out in multiple rooms and are spilling out into the hall in a debaucherous scene. The music blares loud enough to wake whatever dead aren't already up to no good in this godforsaken place.

"You're sure she's on this floor?" I call out, trying to be heard over the noise.

"Looks like she's down that hall somewhere." Chase points in the direction of the bathroom. It occurs to me that one of us should check on Steve's body in the shower stall, but I can't bring myself to suggest it. Chase's eyes flick to the bathroom door as we walk past, which tells me he's thinking the same thing.

We pass our room and Chase jiggles the handle, checking to make sure it's still locked. When he's satisfied, we keep walking.

"I gave her the master key!" I yell. "She was going to look for the cameras."

He nods, eyes on his phone as he walks, so he nearly trips over the splayed-out legs of a shirtless party boy who's wearing a cape and has the words *Captain Penis* written on his chest in Sharpie.

Chase lets out a laugh that is carried away on the bass line.

Whoever pranked this guy also took his pants. I step over

his bare hairy thighs. If it weren't for the steady rise and fall of his chest I'd be concerned for him. But he's breathing, so I guess he's alive, even if he's not doing well. When he sobers up, he should consider getting friends who won't take advantage of him in a vulnerable state.

Chase points down the hall. "Close to here somewhere." His eyes track over the doors ahead of us.

We split up to search rooms. A smoky haze hanging in the air makes it hard to see, so I wind through one room looking in bunk beds and behind closet doors, but there's no sign of Emma. When I step back into the hallway, my eyes have to readjust to the light. Chase emerges, scowling, and shakes his head. He walks to the next door and slips into the darkness. I'm about to cross the hall, but my eyes catch on a utility closet.

There's something on the wood beneath the door handle.

I edge closer, trying to make sense of it. Deep red, almost brown, smeared—

"Blood." The word throbs like an open wound.

I run, not stopping even when I hear Chase call out. I twist the handle and let the door swing wide.

Light streams in to reveal Emma's crumpled body face-down on the floor with a pool of blood under her hips.

"Emmaline!" I scream, dropping to my knees. They slide, smearing blood.

"Don't move her." Chase's trembling voice comes from behind me. "Check her pulse."

I move the curtain of her dirty-blond hair away from her neck and press my fingers to the soft flesh of her throat.

I feel the *tap tap* of her heartbeat, faint, but strong.

She lets out a little moan.

"Emma." I blink and tears drop from my eyes.

Chase is next to us now, looking Emma over cautiously.

"The blood is coming from here," he says, pointing to her lower back. He opens Google and searches *what to do when you're stabbed in the back.*

He scrolls quickly through an article from a medical journal, and then jumps up without a word, grabbing bathroom paper towels and trash bags.

"We need consistent pressure." He hands me the paper towels. "Press that to where the bleeding is."

I apply the paper towels to the spot and hold down, firm and unyielding. This gets me another groan from Emma. Chase ties two trash bags together to make a plastic girdle that we slip under Emma before turning her faceup. Chase knots the trash bags around her like a belt.

Her eyelids flutter open, then closed.

"Emma, hey—hey," I say, pleading. I gently cup her face with one hand. "I can't lose you. Wake up." I touch her neck with my other hand, two fingers checking her pulse, then comb my fingers through her hair, moving the long soft strands away from the blood. "You mean too much to me to lose before I've gotten the chance to figure it out."

Blond eyelashes flutter open, and her lips curl up.

"Tease," she squeaks. Chase laughs through snotty tears.

"Jerk," I say, but all the fire I've got in my voice comes from the gratitude that she managed some snark. I twine my fingers through hers. This time she doesn't pull away.

I hope it means the same thing to her as it does to me.

"The cameras are trashed." Chase grabs the garbage bag

crumpled beside Emma's cracked phone. Good thing her phone still works or we wouldn't have found her. "Shit."

"Chase—" Emma's voice is rough and strained from the effort of speaking, but still strong. He looks at her. He has the number pad on his phone open like he's about to dial.

No matter how afraid we are of what will happen when the cops show up, Emma needs an ambulance.

"Where's Chrissy?" Emma says, swallowing with a wince.

"I don't know, but we need to get you to a hospital. Now." Chase pauses, one finger hovering over the 9.

"I saw . . . him." Emma's eyelids flutter closed.

"Shhh, Emma," I say, and her eyes open again. They settle on mine.

"Not—" she says, pausing to breathe a ragged inhale. "Linda." Emma passes out.

"No—oh my God, Emma, wake up!" I scream. I don't shake her; shaking would only make the bleeding worse. "Chase, this is bad, she's—"

"Kiki." His voice is a razor's edge. I look up into his determined eyes. "You can call the police now."

He drops his eyes, casting one more glance at Emma before he runs from the utility closet.

With trembling fingers, I dial. My pulse pounds way too fast, even as Emma's begins to slow down. The call clicks over.

"Nine-one-one, what is your emergency?"

23

CHRISSY

The phone hasn't stopped buzzing and I'm finally fed up. I yank it out of my pocket to see Chase is calling, again. Bram's fingers close my phone, and he tugs lightly to break it free from my grip. I release it, keeping my eyes focused on the deep cool color of his. I've only been to the ocean a couple of times, but I remember it looked a lot like that. He spins my phone in his hand and declines the call.

"It could be important," I say, but my lips twitch into a smirk to match Bram's. He reaches for my hand, taking the tips of my fingers between his. I let him tug me closer, feeling the heat from his skin ignite the air around us. That gentle hum is there, shutting out all the other thoughts in my head.

"It can wait," he says. He lets go of my hand and reaches up to tuck a few wild strands of my hair behind my ear. His fingers graze the curve of my ear, tripping along my jawline until his thumb reaches my chin. He tugs up.

My lips are positioned perfectly for a kiss.

"They have you all the time," he whispers. "And you're more than just their ghost girl."

Ghost Girl. Chase's original title, before Kiki and Emma joined the channel.

The words slip into the quiet dark crevices of my heart. The secret panels that I hide hurt and anger behind. I am a commodity, but they will never understand me. No matter how they try to, they can't.

"They're my friends." I try to argue, more with my thoughts than with Bram's words.

"I'm your friend, right?" he asks. His eyes drift to my lips and his thumb brushes the soft flesh. "Or am I more than a friend?"

That hum inside my head breaks out across my skin like the buzz of a really good high. I swim in Bram's eyes, dipping deep into the pale cool water. I lean in as my mind blurs, colors and sounds fading away until all I can see, feel, think is him. He is my guide to his lips, drawing my chin up until my mouth fits with his like the last piece of a puzzle.

My lips open to let him explore.

White-hot light fills the darkness behind my closed eyes. Sunlight shoots through soft gray clouds. The curving arms of tree branches become clear.

I hear laughter trailing off. Then the crashing of waves on a shore.

It's a memory, playing for me like a movie.

I twist my hand in Bram's shirt, holding him against me. He likes it. His lips curl up in a smile, but he doesn't break away from our kiss.

The view changes, like someone is rolling onto their side from their back. I see an arm, not as tan or strong as the arm curling around me now, but it's the same one. Long fingers with trimmed nails, that small slim piece of leather tied around the wrist. Bram's arm, Bram's hand, outstretched.

A girl lies on the ground beside him. The tall grass between them blocks most of her from view, but I can see she is wearing a soccer uniform.

The image jolts me. A flash flies through my mind of the dead girl in the pizza parlor.

My lips stiffen against Bram's, but he presses harder, pulls me closer.

Salt and the roar of waves drags me away from Hearst's rooftop again. The waves crash against dark rocks on a sandy shore. Bram cracks the knuckles of his right hand and looks down to the left. Beside him on the rocks is the outstretched unmoving arm of a girl. The tie of her yellow-and-white polka-dot swimsuit is laid out on the rocks beside her.

I push against Bram's chest, and his arms lock around me.

A vise I can't break free from.

Grass sways—I feel it on my skin—and then my eyes open. But it's not my eyes I see through, as it hasn't been this whole time. They're Bram's eyes. And now they—we—stare down at a girl's terrified face.

I recognize her brown eyes and sun-lightened blond hair, the neckline of her T-shirt and the way her two front teeth overlap. I don't have to see *Summer* written on the shirt to know it's the ghost I followed up to the roof.

Bram's hands close around her neck and squeeze *tight, tight, tighter.*

Bruising, crushing, taking.

His feelings surge inside me like a rising tide. Primal, feral, unhinged. *Just take out the trash, just make her stop looking, just stop her from feeling.* She struggles, but she's powerless and he likes that. He likes that she can't resist him, and he holds her life in his hands.

Light fades from her pupils.

I bite down hard on Bram's lip and the pain makes him release me. I taste blood.

I shove him away. I'm shaking all over. My legs want to buckle, and the pain in my head is like a knife slicing through my temple. I reach up with trembling hands to wipe the blood from the top of my lip. I look up, to see Bram's tongue slip out to lick his wound.

A slow evil smile spreads across his face.

My phone sits on the ground between us, buzzing again.

Chase. That stupid pool photo I took is visible above his name.

I lunge to grab my phone just as Bram stomps his hiking boot on top of it. His hand wraps around my wrist, wrenching me away from the phone. He yanks me close to him, and his breath beats against my cheek. His pupils are dilated, but I can still see that clear blue sky, like the summer-day color I liked so much.

He grabs the phone from the ground and launches it off the roof.

"No more interruptions," he says.

24

CHASE

The pin marking Chrissy's location drops off the map.

I keep climbing.

Maybe it's all the time spent in the company of the best psychic in North America, or maybe it's my own intuition kicking in because I care more about her safety than mine right now. My gut screams to go higher. Don't stop or turn back.

Go all the way up.

I know she's alive—I can feel it.

I know she's in danger and there will never be a time I won't be there to help her. No matter what we say to each other. Even if she never likes me back. She never has to be on her own again. She never has to face her nightmares alone in the dark.

I'll always find her.

If I just keep climbing.

I will keep climbing.

25

CHRISSY

Bram has me by the nape of the neck, dragging my body against his. The muscles in his forearm flex and ripple, his blond arm hair standing on end. I stomp down on his toes with the heel of my shoe. He tries to keep holding me, but when I bring my hand across his face in a crackling smack, he lets go.

"Chrissy." He says my name, and it makes my skin crawl. Not with that warm humming high feeling like before. This feels like thousands of tiny centipede legs creeping over my skin. "The Ghost Girl!"

He says it with flair and pizzazz, like he's the ringmaster in a horror hotel circus.

Ghost Girl.

Again.

This time, without the static in my head, I know why it mattered when he said it before.

"Do I know you?" I ask, but the answer hovers in my mind.

"If I kill you will you stay with me forever?" He says it in a mocking tone.

"It's you." I breathe the name of our demented troll.

"Hauntedbyher666, pleasure to meet you," he says, stretching a hand out for a shake. I slap it away.

"You followed us here," I say. It isn't a question. He smiles as an answer anyway.

"Correction," he says, pointing at me, "I followed *you*. I don't give a shit about the others. Not even the cute little go-go girl and her pretty neck."

I feel vomit rise in my throat. I force myself to swallow and keep my expression neutral. I don't want to give him the satisfaction of seeing me flinch.

"You're sick," I say, unemotional. His smile drops.

"Don't you think that's an oversimplification?"

I pretend to consider him carefully. A person like Bram wants recognition, power and control. Killing validates some missing part of his soul.

Broken.

Like a vase cracked down the center held together only by the force of the glass. The shell of his body holds the shards of his soul together, but just barely.

"Nope." I cock one hip. "You're just an unremarkable psychopath who likes to strangle girls to death and leave them to rot."

"Strangle." He shivers. "Such an ugly word for what I do."

"What do you call it?"

"I like to think I set them free." He flutters his fingers toward the sky like a bird taking flight.

My eyes track over to where the ghosts of the *Summer* shirt girl and the one in the polka-dot swimsuit stand beside him.

"They aren't free," I say. Bram follows my eyes, but I can

tell by how his focus doesn't fix on any one spot that he can't see them. Not like I can.

In his momentary distraction, I launch myself toward the fire escape ladder. The burn in my muscles ignites. Adrenaline pumps speed into my legs. My hands close around the curving handles of the rusty metal ladder just as Bram grabs a fistful of hair at the crown of my head and yanks me back. I grip tight to the ladder, using all my strength to pull myself toward it, but the pain in my scalp is unreal, and when he grabs me by the waist, I lose my grip. He throws me to the ground, knocking the wind from my lungs. My vision swims and I know my head is bleeding. The *Summer* shirt ghost peers over his shoulder. She looks at me with kind, sad brown eyes.

Bram gets a grip on both my wrists and holds me down. Just like all the other times he's done this, I feel pleasure slip through him like warm sweet honey.

Fight. The word is in my head.

Fight back.

The swimsuit ghost, her drenched hair dripping tiny drops of salty water on my face, eyes dead and pale and laced through with blood, lies beside me.

Fuck him up.

Her smile is unexpected.

I am more than his victim.

I miss eating Vegemite with my girlfriend at uni.

I was going to be a dancer.

There are multiple voices all around me. I feel them, and even though I can't see them, I know there are more ghosts haunting this story.

Ghost girls with stories of their own that they never got to finish.

Girls like Anna, who died before they were done with the world.

But not me.

I knee Bram in the balls and he buckles.

"Gah!" he wails in pain. His hands release me, and I roll free. He recovers fast, shooting up to block my path, but now I don't want to escape.

I want to face him.

And then, one by one, the girls he killed begin to show me their faces.

26

The sound of sirens is faint and in the distance.

I've been counting the beats of Emma's pulse, watching the shallow movement, up and down, of her chest as she breathes.

I haven't prayed much since my parents sent me to church camp the summer of seventh grade and the pastor told us gays were an abomination, that God is male, and sex before marriage will send us straight to hell.

But God isn't that white man behind the pulpit. God isn't the lies the pastor spewed.

Emma has to make it out of this alive so that I can kiss her at least once and admit to her, and myself, that I've been wanting to for a while.

I whisper prayers into the darkness and hope that somewhere there's a God who cares enough to listen.

One for Emma.

One for Chase.

One for Chrissy.

And then I start over again.

27

CHRISSY

Screaming sirens are growing nearer by the second.

Bram doesn't seem to notice or care. His focus is on me and nothing else. Predatory and precise, he's not going to blink first.

In the moments since I kneed him in the balls I've learned about the girls he killed, and that knowledge helps me understand this murdering teenager from the sticks in Australia.

He's lonely. He has no one to pull him back from the edge, and it's not that I think he deserves that—not with all the horrible things he's done—but it's impossible not to understand the fear of toppling over all alone.

Summer shirt was named Sienna, and she thought Bram wanted to be her boyfriend. She thought he took her out to the meadow to reenact that scene in *Twilight*.

He killed her instead.

Polka-dot bathing suit was taking surf lessons with Bram after school. Her name was Jane.

Naya has black hair and a nose ring. I recognize her soccer uniform from the first time she showed me her face. She sat down behind Bram in the pizza parlor to get my attention. Up close, I can see that her neck has a distinct mark around the center, and when she moves it's clear that her trachea collapsed.

Bastard.

Another girl waited tables someplace called Dolly's. Her name tag says *Deedee*. She's slim and small, with long delicate limbs. Graceful, like the aspiring dancer she was.

"Why would you go to all this trouble, come all this way, to see me?" I ask him. Sienna and Jane are aware of each other more than any ghosts I've come into contact with, but when I look around at the other girls, I can tell they aren't in the know.

They see me. They feel me.

I need them to see each other.

"You see ghosts. I make them," Bram answers simply.

Something serpentine and twisted slithers through my brain. His thought, not mine: he wants me to see his victims because he can't. For some sick reason, he wants to know they're always with him, and maybe that means he's not so alone in the world.

"You kill girls with your bare hands. What makes you think they would follow you around after that?" I ask. "I wouldn't, if I were them." Now it's my turn to smirk. Bram shows me his row of perfect pearly whites in response.

"You'll get your chance to prove it," he says.

As if I'd let him kill me.

"But they do," he continues, like he needs to say it aloud to convince himself. "They brought you up here for me."

The audacity of this guy, wow. Like these ghosts would draw me up to the roof for *him*.

Or maybe they did, only not for the reason he thinks.

"Sienna thought you were going to be her Edward Cullen," I say, and when the name leaves my lips a visible tremor runs through him. He shivers. "She thought your stalker vibes were vampiric in an eternal love sort of way."

"Sienna was my first kill," he says. "Mum died the summer before."

"Oh, so that wasn't a lie?"

"I'm not a liar. Sometimes I bend the truth when it suits me." He shrugs, and the nonchalance of the move makes me want to wring his neck. "If you search my name—my real name"—Chase was right, which doesn't bug me as much as it should—"you'll find my mum's death was quite the spectacle that summer. A bloody awful scene that left two dead. One was the person I loved more than anything else, and the other was the father I despised like the devil. Dear old dad ran us off the road in a rage. I recovered from my injuries." Bram pauses, and his expression softens. "They did not."

His mom isn't among the ghosts shimmering into place beside him.

"She's not here," I say, making sure to keep my focus on his face. "If you were hoping you'd get a chance to say goodbye."

His jaw tightens, the muscles bulging and twitching.

"I bet you see yours all the time." There's a chink showing in his armor now, and I'm not the only one who notices it.

Jane turns her feral gaze to the exposed skin between Bram's hairline and the crew neck of his T-shirt. If she had fangs, she would bite.

"Mine comes around sometimes," I lie, just to hurt him.

His stare turns molten.

"How many are there?" he asks, taking a step toward me. "Count them for me."

"Not a chance."

He takes another step and I flinch. My show of fear unwraps another one of his sinister smiles. He likes to see me squirm, and not just because I'm a worm he has writhing on a hook. I'm alone, isolated from my friends. Isolated like he wanted me to be.

Just like him.

Alone except for the ghosts of the girls whose existence he tried to erase. Alone because I didn't hold my friends close.

Alone.

Not alone. The words shoot through me like a current of electricity.

My fingers tingle and I look down to see a delicate hand, the fingernails filed into perfect ovals and a small gold signet ring with the letter *E* pressed into it, reaching for mine.

Eileen Warren stands beside me. Small-boned and bright-eyed.

She's right.

I'm not alone. And now neither is she.

I turn my gaze from Eileen's, facing Bram again, but I'm not really looking at him. My eyes take in the ghost girls beside him, trapped in the event horizon of the black hole that is his soul.

The last one to come through clearly is Anna.

She was caught in the cross fire, only not Linda and Steve's, not the malicious forces of the Hearst. The rope Bram wrapped around her neck, the life he drained out of her, was all part of his malignant quest to get my attention. Steve, I suppose, was collateral damage.

"There's no way out now, you know?" I say. "My friends have called the cops. I can hear the sirens—"

"Do you think that's because they want to save you from me, or is it because your friend Emma is currently bleeding to death in a storage closet?"

Emma's bleeding out?

Emma.

Bleeding.

Out.

Emma—

The words scramble in my head as a swell of nausea nearly overtakes me.

Eileen's form beside me isn't solid, but it's no less real.

"I never said I expected to make it out of here a free man," Bram says. "I just want to know the answer to one simple question. If I kill you, will you always be with me? Like a puppy dog nipping at my heels."

Ghosts look at you, even when they don't really see you. The pressure of their eyes tracking your energy, shifting with your movement, is tangible.

It's the goose bumps you can't find a reason for.

It's the sluggish feeling in your head when you can't think straight.

It's that chill on a warm summer day.

Sienna's eyes draw the hairs on my arm up like a current. Eileen isn't just near me, she's affecting me. Her energy is making me stronger, and if Eileen can do that, then what's stopping Sienna from reaching out?

Sienna flicks a finger against Bram's ear. He bats it away like a gnat.

"Five," I say. "There are five."

Ten sets of ghost girls' eyes ricochet around searching for the others'.

"Sienna was your first." I repeat what Bram said to me. The left corner of his lip twitches up. "Then Jane, the following summer. Deedee came next, again, in the summer. She was waitressing in Melbourne and you were visiting with your mates." I use her words instead of mine, and the sound of them in my voice makes Bram's features writhe. "Naya was the last one, right before you left for the US. She was pretty and athletic, and she was about to move in with her girlfriend when you picked her up from the soccer field and murdered her under the docks at Port Jackson Bay."

She washed away with the tide and is trapped beside him forever.

Bram is beautiful and charming to any girl he meets. He seems like the perfect friend, boyfriend, soul mate. His disheveled brown hair, deep golden tan and rugged exterior makes everyone look twice without fail. The fact that he could see into the past with a touch and use it to gain girls' trust made him the perfect serial killer.

The ghost girls understand now.

They aren't the only ones who trusted him without thinking twice. They weren't bad or stupid for letting him in. They aren't the reason they died.

He is.

And that's pissing them the hell off.

The temperature on the rooftop plummets.

"But it didn't stop there," I say, letting my eyes trail to Anna.

I feel the cold cuff of Eileen's fingers curl around my wrist. My breath comes in winter smoke even in the dead heat of this Los Angeles All Hallows' Eve.

For the first time, fear assembles like an army in Bram's features.

"Anna was working at Hearst Hotel to put herself through cosmetology school. She had a baby at home and an elderly mother to care for."

Anna looks at the ring on her finger. Her daughter's birthstone.

"And . . ." I pause. The ghost girls press in. "You took her from them."

Jane lunges, hands out, and slams Bram square in the chest, knocking him back into the strong sturdy form of Naya, who has braced herself for the impact.

"What the hell?" Bram says, doubling over in pain as he gulps air. "How did you do that?" He looks at me accusingly, as if I somehow punched him from five feet away. I laugh and glance over my shoulder at Eileen.

Her smile is more alive than Bram's could ever be.

"I didn't do anything, Bram. You wanted to know if they were with you, even in death." My voice is jeering, and I love it. "Well, they're here."

Deedee full-on laughs. The sound is bright, melodic, dancing. The classically trained dancer with the lithe, lean legs and graceful laugh reminds me of gliding across a stage.

Bram's eyes go wide in horror as the sound of her laugh reaches him.

"Isn't this what you always wanted?" I ask. Next to me, Eileen twines her fingers with mine.

Naya grabs Bram around the neck, dragging him toward the edge of the roof. Sienna punches him square in the gut as Jane and DeeDee each take an arm. Anna approaches, and with one strong kick she knocks Bram's legs out from beneath him.

"Stop them, please!" Bram screams, his lips quivering. His eyes plead. "Don't let them—"

Jane uses two fingers to jab at his eyes. Naya joins her, and together they tug him to the edge of the roof. He struggles, unable to see them and fight back.

He's begging them now.

"Please, don't do this—I loved you—all of you—I love you. . . ."

Sienna falters, her grip slipping as his words come out rapid fire. She had wanted him to love her then and he didn't. She knows he didn't. She was trash; she was nothing.

Bram uses his free hand to grab the ladder railing.

Sienna opens her mouth to scream.

One by one, each ghost girl screams. The chorus of their rage harmonizes with the backdrop of city sounds and sirens. I join in, and as I scream, I feel Eileen's cold hand leave mine.

She moves as if in fast-forward over the ground between us and the killer. Her eyes track over the other ghost girls. Her lips open, electric gears sounds screech from her mouth—the sound of her death forever on her lips. She grips Bram by the wrist and wrenches his hand from the railing.

I wish he could see her satisfied smile.

She looks at Anna, who steps up with one finger pointed

and presses it hard into Bram's forehead, launching him over the edge.

The sirens screech into the street below, drowning out the sound of Bram's scream.

I drop to my knees. Light slices through my vision and my skull feels like it's about to split open and spill my brains all over the cement. Blood trickles from my nose, dripping to the ground. When I open my eyes, I see that one of the ghost girls has set my beanie within arm's reach. I pick it up and slowly pull it down over my forehead and ears.

When I look up, I'm alone again.

28

CHASE

The door to the roof is locked. I can hear Chrissy screaming, but weirdly, it doesn't sound like just she is screaming. It's like there are others with her. Girls screaming, all together. Almost as one.

I pound my fists against the metal door, rattling its hinges. I'll kill Bram if he hurts her. Somehow, I'll find a way.

Or—*let's be real*—I'll probably have to let the authorities take him away in cuffs and eviscerate him on the witness stand. Even my rage won't enable me to take him in a physical altercation.

If he hurts her, I'll never forgive myself for being the idiot who couldn't put his own bullshit down long enough to be a good friend to the person I care most about on the whole stupid planet.

The screaming stops. Now all I can hear is the sound of sirens.

Screw this—I run to the window that looks out from the stairwell onto the street and edge up to try to get a glimpse below. The glass is covered with city grime, and the ground is far away, but I can make out the shape of a body. The limbs are all twisted and mangled from a long fall, but from here I can't tell who it is.

The creak of rusted hinges startles me, and I turn around to see the door slowly open.

I take a deep breath because I don't know what I'll find on the other side of the door and I'm scared. I'm the most terrified I've ever been in my life.

I take the few steps left to get to the roof, and exhale a huge gasp of relief when I see her, Chrissy, crouched on the ground, alone. She looks up, eyes tracking across the roof searching for the sound she just heard. They lock on me and her face crumples. Her shoulders start to shake and she closes her eyes, dropping her face into her hands.

My feet move, one in front of the other, until I'm sprinting across the roof. I drop to my knees in front of her, but don't touch her. I just look for signs of damage. Her lips are smeared with blood. Her elbows are scraped, and there are granules of concrete embedded in them.

She drifts forward, grabbing onto my T-shirt and pressing her forehead against my chest. I hold her, letting her cry for a few solid seconds, and it's stupid that the thought that enters my head is how natural it feels to have her in my arms. I force my mind to focus all the energy I have left on Chrissy, on what she needs and not what this means to me.

She stops crying, lets out a few final sniffles and pulls back to look at me. Her eye makeup streaks black down her cheeks. I show her my thumb and she nods, lifting her face toward me so I can wipe away her tears and mascara. She watches me the whole time, and I can feel her prodding me psychically for information. She wants clues to my thoughts. She wants answers, and she definitely expects an apology.

"Your relief feels like a cool gust of air on a hot day," she says. I feel the edge of my upper lip kick up.

"I'm sorry I acted like a dick," I say.

"You were right about him."

"That's not an excuse."

"Nope," she says, wiping at her nose, but it doesn't do any good. The blood is caked on.

"Bram?" I ask.

"Street pancake." She shakes her head and her eyes trail to the edge of the roof, then back to me. "I had help. Guardian angels. Lots of them." Her eyes drift over my shoulder and fix on something. I know enough now about the Ghost Girl to know that I don't need to look behind me. I won't ever see what she does.

She smiles and looks at me again. "You had help too."

"Okay?" I smirk. I'll follow up on that later. And just as fast as her smile appeared, it vanishes.

"Emma," she says, and grabs me by the arms. Her hands are cold despite the heat, and I feel a jolt of electricity where they touch my skin.

"Bram stabbed her, but I don't know how she is because . . ." I pause. I have to work up the courage. I'm about to get vulnerable and it's not going to be pretty. "I ran to find you. I know you're fully capable of taking care of yourself in the face of a murdering psychopath, but God, Chrissy, you're my best friend, and not just because of the channel—forget the channel—you mean more to me than the Gold Play Button or a billion subs ever could and I couldn't live with myself—"

Her lips crush against mine, which are open in midsentence, but holy shit this is unreal.

Chrissy Looper is kissing me.

I taste blood and I don't care. I kiss her back with everything in me.

"It's weird when you use my full name," she says against my lips. I try to defend myself, but can't because she works her lips against mine and damn it if I don't comply.

...

CHRISSY

Kissing Chase isn't like kissing any other boy. Ever.

His lips are soft and yielding, and he lets me lead the way even though most of the time in our normal lives he's the one calling the shots. I could get used to how his joy feels pulsing through me, like sunlight breaking through clouds after rain. I could get used to how his hands press carefully and cautiously but still hungrily on the curve of my waist.

It's only when he needs a breath that we separate and finally stand up.

"We have a lot of explaining to do," he says, holding on to me like he never, ever wants to let go. "The whole moving-Steve's-body thing isn't great." His eyes droop in concern as he looks at me. "What *exactly* happened to Bram?"

"He was hauntedbyher666," I say, and the chill from the ghosts slips over my skin again.

Chase's eyes bug out. "That bastard."

"And Anna wasn't his first kill, not even close. I expect when I give details to the cops, they'll be able to help the Australian police solve a string of unsolved murders."

"And you could see all of them?" Chase asks, amazed.

"All of them and then some," I say. Something tugs at the edges of my awareness. I turn.

Eileen stands across the rooftop, alone.

She's backlit by the lights of downtown Los Angeles. Her thumbs are tucked into the belt loops of her low-slung jeans.

Her gaze drifts to Chase, then back to me.

Eileen faced the horrors of the Hearst Hotel all on her own, and they broke her. We may never know exactly why or how she died. But I do know that she's spending her afterlife helping the souls who find themselves stuck here. Just like she did tonight.

Unlike Eileen, I'm not alone. The hotel drove us to the breaking point, but it didn't break us. It couldn't because, even when we're idiots, the first rule of the Ghost Code is never go anywhere alone. Even when we splintered, we didn't break apart.

Whatever we face next, we know we have each other and we can do anything together.

Eileen waves to me. I whisper goodbye to her. She slips over the edge of the roof and vanishes.

"You wanna hold my hand while we walk down the stairs?" I ask Chase.

"Every damn time." He fits our fingers together.

I'm not alone.

Not now. Not ever.

Ghost Girl started as a girl doing readings in living rooms and searching haunted locations for spirits no one else could see. But it was always supposed to be about us.

The four of us.

Kiki, the scaredy-cat with a backbone of steel.

Emmaline, the sarcastic tech geek with a heart of gold.

Chase, the visionary with Walk of Fame dreams.

And me.

The psychic with a dark side longing to come into the light.

EPILOGUE

" 'Posers'!" Chase grumbles.

His cursor hovers over one of the thousands of comments on the most recent video.

Location: Winchester Mystery House

Event: My first public reading since the events at Hearst Hotel

We sold tickets because our new managers—excuse me while I vomit everywhere—insisted. We had to turn people away.

"Haters gonna hate," Kiki says, dropping down onto the sofa beside Emma. She runs her tongue along the edge of an ice cream cone and takes a big lick of strawberry cheesecake into her mouth.

"Ignore, ignore," Emma says, reaching over Kiki's shoulder and tugging her in for a snuggle. They've been dating for a few months, but only in the last couple of weeks have they started PDAing all over the pool house. Kiki offers her the ice cream cone and Emma takes a bite.

Six months later, and pretty much everything has changed.

For starters, Chase is totally obsessed with UPS's delivery schedule.

"They said it would be delivered by four p.m.," he says, spinning around in his chair and holding his phone out in front of him.

"Dude," Emma says.

"Friend," Kiki interjects. Emma leans over, positioning her face below Kiki's lips.

"He's male, babe," Emma says, batting her lashes at Kiki, who slaps her baseball cap down over her eyes in annoyance. Emma howls with laughter and shoves the cap back up, spinning it around backward.

Her eyes say everything that's in her heart.

You're magnificent.

You're my everything.

I want more ice cream.

She tugs Kiki in for another kiss.

I chuckle, and Kiki and Emma shoot me a look. "What?" Kiki asks.

I say, "Oh, um, Emma wants more ice cream."

The pillow in my face is a good-natured warning. *Get the hell out of my head, Chrissy.*

All right, all right.

Emma was in the hospital for weeks recovering from the surgery necessary to patch up her stab wound. She's proud of her gnarly scar and even showed it off on Zoom for the Ghost Gang's *Today* show interview.

I look over at Chase, who's incessantly refreshing the browser window on his phone. We walked down together to face the police. By the time we arrived at the scene, Bram's body had been covered by a white sheet, like a bedsheet ghost.

They wrapped us in those gray wool blankets like in the

movies. They gave me first aid for my head wound, which was shallow and didn't even need stitches.

They asked minimal questions. We knew there would be more. From the cops, and district attorneys, journalists and parents. But at that moment we were traumatized children. Except for Chase, who was a traumatized legal adult.

They carted Linda out in handcuffs even though she wasn't the one who killed Steve or Anna. Turns out, she had other dirty dealings going on. With help from her doormat (and now dead) offspring Steve, Linda had been stealing from residents and guests of the Hearst for years. Years of back taxes and un-paid debts meant she couldn't get a loan to do the necessary repairs on the hotel, and after trying all the legal channels, she resorted to thievery. She knew the type of person who'd stay at the Hearst wasn't the kind the police would take seriously when they reported missing money or belongings.

As Linda was shoved into the back of a squad car, I saw Steve watching from a lobby window. He was still dressed in his Hearst Hotel uniform, hat askew ever so slightly, empty gray eyes searching the street for something to latch onto. Steve would have loved to make his mom happy, but never got the chance. I didn't outright ask him if he was planning to move on from the hotel, but somehow I knew there was no way he ever could.

The Hearst had claimed him, and it doesn't let go easily.

"Finally! Yes!" Chase exclaims, shooting up from his chair. He drops his gaze briefly to mine. "Be right back."

"Don't say that," Kiki groans. "People always say that in slasher movies and they never come back."

"We're not in a horror movie, not anymore!" Chase shouts over his shoulder. "Now it's a romance!"

"Excuse me while I hurl," Emma says, making a gagging noise before finishing the last bite of Kiki's ice cream.

The channel exploded after our fateful trip to Hearst Hotel. Media coverage came fast and abundant. Everywhere we looked someone was asking for a selfie. We were on all the morning talk shows, reliving the events of that night until we were numb to them and Kiki refused to comply anymore because trauma press wasn't really her thing, and I got tired of cameras not operated by Chase being shoved in my face.

Emma's scholarships came through for MIT and Stanford, and yesterday we celebrated with a three-tiered cake covered in maroon frosting. She leaves at the end of the summer, and Kiki's off to Berkeley, so they plan to do a semi-long-distance thing, but my money is on one of them caving and transferring.

Probably Emma.

"I can't believe we graduate in less than a month," Kiki says. "How is that even real?"

"Four years at Ridgeway High," Emma says. "Get me the hell out."

"I won't miss it," I say. "But I'll miss you guys."

"*Humans,*" Emma and Kiki say in unison, and I stick my tongue out at them.

"Jesus. Like Chase doesn't have every three-day weekend and holiday already booked."

"Like he hasn't scheduled us all for filming locally any time he can squeeze it in." Emma rolls her eyes and shoots up from the couch, then walks over to the fridge for a Fanta.

"It won't be the same, and you know it," I call after her. "And you'll miss it too."

"We have the summer!" Kiki says. I can tell she's frustrated. She doesn't want things to change. It's all happening so fast.

"You're right, we have every summer," I point out for Kiki's benefit. Her whole body relaxes.

The pool and a hiatus, finally. We took a few weeks off for the media blitz and Emma's recovery, but we still posted on social media, and every single time we did, more subscribers poured into YouTube. Chase has spent the last six months obsessively watching that ticker go up on the Ghost Gang home page.

The door bursts open and Chase shuffles in holding a cardboard box with the YouTube logo. His knuckles are white with excitement and he grips the box like it's the Holy Grail. He walks to the center of the room and drops down on the ottoman, setting the box in front of him.

"Chrissy, do you wanna do the honors?" he asks.

"Chase," I say, loving the way his name feels on my lips, "this is your baby. You do it."

"This is *our* baby," he says, looking at all of us. "It belongs to all of us. We did this together."

"Okay, it's not a baby, it's a cheap plastic trophy," Emma groans. "Can we get on with it, please? Kiki and I have dinner plans."

"Anniversary." Kiki does the most adorable shimmy of joy.

"Of what?" Chase asks, his expression quizzical.

Emma just smirks.

"Open the box," I say, widening my eyes ever so slightly.

"Right," he says, exhaling. "This is it."

He slides his hands into the box and breathes out and then in.

After six months, Chase and I are still going strong. He's not a guy you date and break up with. He's not a passing ship in the night. He's the endgame boy. The one you make your dad be nice to at dinner, even if dinner is only Kentucky Fried Chicken. He's the boy you tell every secret to in the quiet of night and under the blanket of a million stars in the Mojave Desert. He's the boy you trust without question, that you question without fear. He's the one for me, and I know it, but he doesn't know it. Yet.

He pulls the plaque out and the light catches on the gold plate.

PRESENTED TO

𝕿𝖍𝖊 𝕲𝖍𝖔𝖘𝖙 𝕲𝖆𝖓𝖌

FOR PASSING 1,000,000 SUBSCRIBERS

We hit that milestone two weeks after the events at the Hearst Hotel, and without looking at the channel stats today I can guarantee we're seconds away from closing in on two.

Chase reached his goal.

But by the time he hit it, he didn't even seem to care.

(He did, but he loves to pretend he doesn't. So I humor him.)

Chase holds the Gold Play Button up for a photo and Kiki proceeds to micromanage everything until it's perfect. She's taken on a much bigger role behind the scenes while also managing every element in front of the camera. She's the only one willing to talk to the management team, and the only one, besides me, most people request to always be present at a Ghost Gang interview outside the channel.

"We did it." Chase beams.

"Yay, thank you, psycho killer!" Emma jokes. The gang goes silent.

They all look at me.

The one subject we never touch is Bram, Roy, whatever his name was.

But six months later I can honestly say:

"Rest in peace, Bram." I raise a sneaky brow. "Or in hell if that suits you better."

We all lift our voices in a cheer. Chase stands, stretching, and his eyes land on my lips.

"Movie night?" he asks.

"Absolutely." I stand too.

His kiss sends a jolt down my spine.

The others chatter as they file out of the pool house, turning off lights and giggling into the growing dark. I'm the last one left inside. I stare at the Gold Play Button on the ottoman and remember everything we went through to get here. Even though none of this happened according to plan, we still rallied and re-grouped to work from our pain and not be destroyed by it.

I turn off the computer screen, its low cool light taking all the color from the room. It's just me and the empty clubhouse, and french doors that open out to the pool, backed by a vivid Las Vegas sunset.

Only, that's not true.

Not now. Not ever.

I'm never alone now, and never will be again.

Through the window I see him, wearing the same clothes he had on the night he fell to his death from the rooftop of the Hearst Hotel. His lips curl up in a smirk, not a smile—never a smile. He waves, leather bracelet still on his wrist. For a second I feel that familiar, uncomfortable pang that's always been there when I see a ghost.

The dead and the living don't coexist in harmony.

Sometimes the dead want help. Other times they just want to scare you or show you how they died.

And sometimes they just don't want to be alone.

But you know what? I don't care what they want anymore. Now they come to me on my terms. This is my life.

It's up to me how I live it.

I may see ghosts, but that doesn't mean I'm haunted by them.

ACKNOWLEDGMENTS

The origin story of this book still feels like a fever dream—one we don't ever want to wake up from. *Horror Hotel* came from a shared passion for haunted locations, slasher films and true crime, but what wound up on the page was a story that is not only profoundly close to our hearts, but also exactly what we wanted to read when we were two teenage girls growing up with Hollywood on the brain.

The fever dream (or "Five-Day Book Deal" as we're known to call it) began with a tweet from Vice President of Delacorte Press Wendy Loggia calling on writers to send her their best, most commercial and consumable proposals for YA horror, romance and thrillers. Thank you, Wendy, for the opportunity to write in your presence. We are truly thrilled to be here. To our editor, Alison Romig: your genius ideas and clear editorial insights have helped shape this concept from a gripping proposal written in five days to the beautiful piece of art it is now. Thank you for how you have shepherded this book into the world with us.

To our superstar agent, Katie Shea Boutillier: thank you, x3000. Without you jumping on board for this wild ride, we would not be writing these words today. Your guidance and stellar commercial taste helped drive this story from concept to execution. When we came to you with the idea of going all in on a high-concept YA horror proposal, you didn't blink. You asked all the right questions, as always, and never once doubted we could do it.

The beauty you, dear reader, hold in your hands would not be as stunning without the incredible design team at Underlined, and our fiercely talented cover artist, David Seidman. We are in the very best hands as we launch this book into the world. We feel so incredibly lucky.

Eight years ago, we were baby writers who both had the brilliant idea to take Nova Ren Suma's first-ever YA workshop. That's where we met and discovered that we were both super-cool people with big dreams. Thank you, Nova, for our incredible online meet-cute and for encouraging our writing all this time!

Thank you, Demetra Brodsky, for supporting this book from the get-go. A special thank-you goes out to Sara Biren, who read the first forty pages of that fever dream proposal (in hours!) when we weren't sure what the alphabet even was anymore. And to Liz Parker, who sent us a screenshot of Wendy's tweet and said, "You two should do this." She was correct, and we would never have known about it if not for her.

FAITH

To my husband and son, who put up with my ramblings about ghosts and murder and let me watch all the horror movies because "I need to stay in the mindset," I adore you beyond measure. Nathan, thank you for making me dinner, bringing me martinis, and beaming with love as I shine. Sam, thank you for watching hours of *Modern Family* when I need a break and snuggles when I'm exhausted and for always keeping me humble. You two believed in my talent and drive, sometimes even more than I did. You have earned your bragging rights.

Thank you, my Beez: Sara, Liz, and Tracey, who also put up with my ramblings, just via group text instead. Emily and Austin, your friendship means the world to me—agent sibs forever! Kayla, thank you for all the writing sprints. Hannah West, for telling me that story about Rick Ramirez. And Jenny, for Italian dinners and talks by the swimming pool, and being part of my LA family.

Thank you, Dad, for raising me to trust my own psychic sense, and Mom for teaching me how to be brave in the face of anything. I come from a family of big, brash human beings with dark and twisty pasts who learned to heal through telling stories. Thank you, Uncle Keith, for teaching me that exaggeration is the key to a good yarn.

V, years ago you asked me if I wanted to write a book together and I said yes. Best. Idea. Ever. Thank you for inviting me on this journey—it's the most fun I've ever had. Aries #1 forever, you are my truest tiger friend, a sister I didn't know I needed, and the best partner a girl could have.

VICTORIA

To my momma, who is always my first reader. Your love and support are why I am here; they're the magic carpet I use to ride through life.

And Daddy! Who was so proud of me that one time I beat you at checkers. Thank you for being a sucker for me.

To Nick, thank you for putting up with my true-crime obsession, even though sometimes it scares me, and then I can't sleep and poke you awake and ask you if you have anxiety because I have anxiety. You are my love.

Jenny—Nick would have gotten mad if I put you before him, but you are my best friend in the whole wide world, and I honestly don't know what I'd do without you. Thank you for always telling me you "have a feeling this is going to work" even though you actually have no clue.

Geo—thank you for always being excited about my author things, even though you don't really like to read that much. :) Just kidding! Thank you for being a walking encyclopedia and for having the best book recs on the planet. To the Roman Empire!

To Aunt Paige, the entire Rollins clan (Regina, Richard, Chris, Alex, BR, Cesar, Linda, Dave), Leslie, Mary Jane, Tim, Jess, Amber, Sofia, Beth, Theresa, Alyssa, Janet, Pilar: thank you for cheering me on, even when it was still just small potatoes! The potatoes are getting bigger!

To Faith, what a wild ride this has been! You are my story-loving, whiskey-drinking Scorpio soul mate ("you're not a bat"), and writing with you is a dream come true. I've never known anyone to love writing as much as you do. Can't wait for more deadlines in more haunted hotels!

THEY WANT YOU.

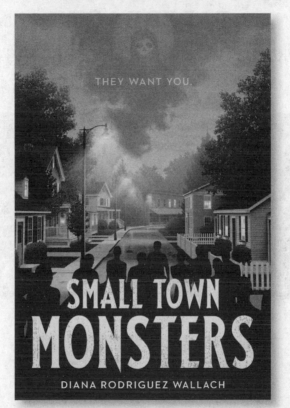

TURN THE PAGE FOR A PREVIEW OF ANOTHER UP-ALL-NIGHT HORROR STORY FROM UNDERLINED!

CHAPTER ONE

Vera

A darkness surged through Roaring Creek, casting a shadow upon its modest homes and oozing onto Vera Martinez's hands—and it all began, at least for her, the day that Maxwell Oliver's pale brown eyes turned her way.

He was staring.

Vera flipped a fistful of curls in front of her face and pretended not to notice. This was an unfamiliar situation. Boys never looked at Vera, and certainly not like this.

She opened an eight-hundred-page novel, reduced to the five-inch screen on her phone, and pretended to read. Discreetly, she scratched her scalp with a nail chipped of black polish and let her gaze slip between her wavy strands. Yup, he was still looking.

"All right, class!" Ms. Spuhler cleared her throat to begin their last day of eleventh-grade English. "Settle down." The teacher grabbed the TV remote, the only tool necessary on the final day of classes.

Roaring Creek High School had the feel of an iPhone powering down one app at a time. Science teachers cleaned lab equipment, jocks threw out ratty sneakers, and theater kids sobbed over the end of another magical season. Vera, however, was the app that no one clicked. She was "Keynotes" or "Numbers," an icon you couldn't delete due to manufacturer settings but was rarely engaged.

So why was Maxwell Oliver suddenly taking notice?

"We'll be picking up *Jane Eyre* right where we left off," said Ms. Spuhler. So far today, Vera had watched *Saving Private Ryan* in AP History; *Hidden Figures* in precalculus; and now *Jane Eyre* in Advanced English.

He's not looking at me, she reasoned. Then, because she had to prove herself right, Vera glanced at the window behind her, expecting to see a flying squirrel or mating robins drawing Maxwell's attention. But there was nothing. Not even a breeze.

Her brow furrowed. Vera and Maxwell had never spoken, not directly, or at least if they had, she couldn't remember it. They'd never been partners on a project or run into each other at the beach. To say they moved in different social circles would imply that Vera had a circle, which she didn't. Unless you counted her family, and that was just sad. Vera preferred to be thought of as sans-circle. The loner. The outcast. The . . . well, all the other names that people called her.

Her parents had *unconventional* careers, the kinds that caused dog walkers to cross the street when they passed the Martinez home and mothers to refuse to let their children go over for playdates. Vera had long since accepted this, because what other choice did she have? Hating her reality would mean hating her mom and dad, and she refused to go there.

Maxwell Oliver, on the other hand, was an athlete, an honest-to-goodness *I competed in the Junior Olympics* sprinter. He was beloved. Janitors high-fived him in the hallway, and girls, if given the option, would line up in formal wear for a chance to accept his thornless rose.

Vera was different, for a slew of reasons that added up to her not being the type who'd catch Maxwell Oliver's eye. Yet he was *staring*, almost like he had something to say. It made no sense. Every cell in her brain screamed *Don't fall for it, it's a trick!* But still her stomach twisted with the toxic taste of hope. A shoved-down piece of her soul longed for someone to look at her and see something other than the five-year-old everyone avoided on the playground.

Vera tucked a thick lock of hair behind her ear and gnawed on her lip. She was under no obligation to pretend she didn't notice. *He* was staring at *her*. So technically *he* should be embarrassed.

She steadied herself, preparing to meet his gaze head-on. What was the worst that could happen? After today, she wouldn't see Maxwell again until the start of senior year.

Vera inhaled, summoning all her courage from down deep, when Jackson Johnson stumbled into the classroom. He tripped in a walloping belly flop onto the linoleum floor, and the room erupted into laughter. Jackson immediately bounced up, milking the crowd with his arms spread in a victorious V. "We're almost out of heeeere!" he shouted.

Applause broke out, everyone whooping and giggling as he danced about as if in a training montage. Even Vera chuckled as she stole another peek at Maxwell. His gaze still lingered, lips parted, and he was prepared to mouth something. Then both his friends abruptly turned her way. They whispered, chuckled, clearly talking about her. Vera's cheeks flushed, and she let her eyes flit about the room until the heat in her face subsided. When she glanced back, Maxwell's focus hadn't shifted. Only, before he could speak, Jackson snatched a notebook and smacked Maxwell on the top of his head. Ms. Spuhler dimmed the classroom lights.

And the moment was shattered.

But it *had been* a moment. Vera was certain of it.

She just didn't know what it meant.

She would soon.

The darkness hanging over Roaring Creek was inching closer to Vera Martinez.

And it all began with a single look.